COLTER SONS BOOK 5

THE RESTLESS WRANGLER

Karen Baney

desert life
media

The Restless Wrangler: Colter Sons Book 5
By Karen Baney

Publisher:
Desert Life Media, LLC
Gilbert, AZ 85295

www.karenbaney.com

Printed in the United States of America

ISBN-979-8-9863369-5-4

The Lord watches over the sojourners;
he upholds the widow and the fatherless,
but the way of the wicked he brings to
ruin.

—Psalm 146:9

CHAPTER 1

My name is Preston Colter. I lived the first eight years of my life enjoying my status as the baby of the family. Everyone loved me. I was cute. I was funny.

Then Violet came along to dethrone me. Everyone always says that Sam is Mama's favorite. He was, but only before Violet's birth. She is the one and only Colter daughter, holding a position of eternal affection in my mama's heart. A fifth son just can't compete with that.

So, in my sorrow, I turned to horses. I started hanging out at Larson's Stables. Uncle Adam put me to work mucking stalls as soon as I was big enough to hold a shovel. It was fine. Anything in life that is worth doing comes with some sort of mess attached to it. At least, that's what the first seventeen years of my life taught me.

I didn't mind the hard work of breaking and training the horses. I loved it. Sure, my backside hurt more than a time or two.

Then, as I turned eighteen, my thoughts turned inward. I was jealous of my older brothers. Both James and Boone received blessing after blessing. Everything they did was successful. My parents definitely loved them more than me, the forgotten son. Sam made Papa proud the moment he embraced taking over Colter Ranch. He solidified his posi-

1

tion in Papa's esteem when he married the perfect Ellie Mae.

Even the oddball Deacon made my parents proud by pursuing a steady career that my sort of adopted brother, Grady Thatcher, also pursued.

Speaking of Grady, he was the other person to usurp any positive standing I had with my parents. I only wanted to be seen. The moment Grady came to live with us, I stood no chance of making my mark. He instantly befriended Deacon, stealing the place I held as Deacon's trusted confidant. He earned my parents' respect and was the perfect son my parents wished I was.

So, I embraced my role in the family—the moody, rebellious son. It was the only role that garnered me attention, albeit negative attention. It didn't matter to me. They finally saw me. Seen enough that a few years ago, Mama sent me with Boone on one of his surveying expeditions to straighten me out.

No one asked if I wanted to straighten out. No one asked what I wanted from the family, or even from life. They just wanted a good Christian son that would not tarnish their reputation. So, I determined to give them the exact opposite.

I became a saddle bum. Restless. Reckless. I cared little for much besides horses and a mediocre bottle of whiskey. For several years, I worked as a wrangler on one ranch or another in northern Arizona until I drank too much and got fired. It didn't matter. I sobered up until I got the next job. My pattern repeated itself.

Little did I know the trip to Ash Fork with Boone's expedition would change my life in unfathomable ways. It took me a few years to realize it. But looking back, those nights with the lovely Hetty Clark changed her life and mine forever.

But I'm getting ahead of myself. My story starts with one pivotal night where I should have died. Only I didn't. Instead, a chain reaction of events ignited that led to the biggest shock of my young life.

CHAPTER 2

Ash Fork, Arizona Territory
April 24, 1893

PRESTON

It was too early in the day to start drinking. But there I sat, eager to begin.

"What brings you in so early?" the bartender asked.

I grunted and slapped a coin on the counter. He poured my drink of choice, which he already knew, as I was a regular. I would not tell him they fired me again.

Didn't matter. I would land on my feet soon enough. I always did.

In the meantime, I drank to numb the hurt and pain that constantly nipped at my heels. The drink never failed to deliver on its promise to absorb the pain and make me invincible again. There's a reason some folks call it liquid courage, and I understood it firsthand.

I lost track of time, as was typical when I was between jobs, so to speak. Other patrons entered the saloon.

"It's here," one man said to no one in particular as he sat on the barstool next to me. "The Santa Fe, Prescott, &

Phoenix train arrived this afternoon. First one all the way from Prescott."

After I chugged the last of my whiskey, I nodded to the bartender for a refill. I was pretty sure my oldest brother, James, was involved with that railroad. His touch was better than Midas's.

The man continued to talk, but I ignored him. I staggered to a table to escape his chattering.

When I slid onto a chair, one of the saloon girls started getting friendly. She touched my chest, and I removed her hand. I was such a regular that she should have known I would decline. Don't know why that night in particular she thought I might behave differently.

I had only been with one woman, and she wasn't no prostitute. She was the love of my life. No other woman would ever hold any appeal besides Hetty Clark.

And I knew it from the first time I met her at the Cowboy Tournament on Independence Day in 1889. It was the first time I'd seen a woman dressed in britches. Not a split skirt like my Aunt Julia. Hetty wore a plaid shirt and denim pants, just like a man.

Except no one would mistake her for a man. Her curvy figure and long blond braid left no doubt as to her gender. At seventeen, she was all woman.

Then I saw those sparkling green eyes and her sassy, confident smile. She was there to ride broncos. I teased her it was a man's sport.

She laughed with that beautiful silky voice of hers tinged with arrogance. "Then why are you competing? You're just a boy, judging by your lanky limbs."

I was hooked from that moment on.

She won first place that year. 'Course that was first place out of five women. Still, it was an accomplishment.

Then Hetty came to watch me compete. I won first place too. Out of thirty men. I rubbed it in her face.

"Whatcha think about that? First out of thirty."

"Not bad for a *boy*."

We had been in the solitude of the barn, so I pulled her against me and kissed her senseless. She was the first woman I kissed. But I could tell she enjoyed it.

Then I walked away. Left her standing there.

She sought me out the next day to tease me some more. I kissed her again, and she ensnared my heart.

Before I knew it, she went back home to her family's ranch in Ash Fork, leaving me behind in Prescott to dream of when I might see her again.

The next year, we picked up right where we left off. I won first place again. So did she. We celebrated with lots of kissing before she returned to her family ranch yet again.

That was the year I embraced my bad-boy nature. I started drinking with cowboys from Colter Ranch on our days off. By the time December came around, I was a regular scoundrel, or so my family told me.

No one knew I only partook in the vices called alcohol and cigarettes. Didn't matter. I liked the reputation I built. It got me the attention I so desperately craved.

Then Mama got it in her mind that I needed to sober up. She sent me north with Boone. Where did we end up? Ash Fork.

The best part of the trip was the few days I spent hiding out in the barn at Hetty's ranch. I drank plenty, but Hetty joined me late at night. We got little shuteye those nights as we ignored all proper boundaries and reveled in each other. That encounter proved to her I was most definitely a man.

I sighed as my thoughts turned away from the memories of Hetty Clark. The calico queen tried a few more times to coax me away from my drink and my table. I continued to refuse her.

Before I could blink, a man yanked me out of my chair, and he dragged me outside.

"You keep your hands off my girl!"

My sufficiently numbed brain couldn't make sense of who his girl was until the soiled dove joined us in the street.

"Leave him alone!" she yelled at the large man with arms as thick as my two combined.

I squared up, sort of. Wasn't much stability in my stance, as numb as I was. I readied myself for the fight. I'd been in enough to read the signs that one was coming.

Sure enough, enormous arms swung at my face. The force of it caused my head to turn and my feet to slide out from under me. I landed hard on the ground.

When I sat up, he kicked me in the stomach. Then he hauled me to my feet and landed another few fists in my stomach, back, and face.

As the saloon girl left the scene, the world felt entirely un-stable.

Then enormous arms dragged me down the street by the feet. Rocks would have sliced my shirt had I not been wearing my tan leather duster. He continued pulling me away from the saloon. Then he shoved me into the back room of a building.

"You shouldn't have gone after my girl!"

After another punch, I curled up in a ball on the floor. He closed the door behind him. The lock clicked into place.

Between the drinking and the beating, my energy was gone, so I succumbed to sleep.

Sometime later, I woke to the smell of smoke. My body ached, and the blissful numbness of the drink left me. I sat up as thick smoke stung my eyes.

I crawled toward the door and grabbed the knob. It didn't budge. He locked me in a room with no windows. No hope of escape.

"Help!"

I yelled out as I pounded on the door. No answer came.

As the reality of my situation became clear, desperation settled over me. I didn't really want to die. Certainly not by burning to death. I was only twenty-two.

Some distant memory from my childhood came to mind. Mama told me that God would never leave me. Most of my adult life I spent trying to test that theory. But in that locked room filled with smoke, I decided it might be worth a shot.

"God, if you get me outta this, I'll change. I'll be a better man."

That was it. One half-hearted promise to be different.

The smoke grew thicker. I panicked as flames licked the door.

Then all the sudden, the door splintered. A man entered the room. He rescued me.

"You alright?" he asked as we stumbled to the ground.

I had no voice and started coughing.

"Anyone else in there?"

I shrugged.

Then he ran back into the burning building. Before he returned, a loud crack sounded above me. I watched in horror as the roof collapsed onto the man who had just saved my life.

As I crawled on my hands and knees away from the burning building, I saw the entire town engulfed in flames.

My head throbbed. I reached up and felt crusted blood. My energy left me and I laid down in the middle of the street and closed my eyes.

———

The next morning, I woke lying next to a group of injured people. I started to sit up, but powerful hands pushed me back down.

"Stay still," a man's deep voice commanded. "Doc thinks you have a concussion. Don't get up. Just rest."

"The man?" I asked.

He shook his head.

I frowned. What kind of God sends a man to rescue a rogue like me, then lets him die in the fire? In my place. It should have been me. I had done little of value with my wretched life.

"What's your name, son?"

"Preston."

"My name's Clyde. Clyde Caldwell."

"Sir."

"Let me see if I can't scrounge up some water for you."

Clyde left. Then he returned a few minutes later with a mug of cool water. I drank it down. That's when I noticed the sharp pain in my gut.

"Looks like you got beat up before the fire last night."

I nodded. "Think it was a fight outside the saloon, though it's a mite fuzzy for me."

"You feel up to walking?"

"I suppose."

"Good. Iris, that's my wife, and I decided you should come stay with us until you're fully recovered."

A dozen people around me suffered worse injuries. I did not understand why the man and his wife were helping me.

Exhaustion stopped me from thinking about it. I accepted their help and fell into the bed they provided. Just before sleep tugged at the corners of my consciousness, I recalled my promise. God certainly got me out of that fire. I wondered just what kind of change He might require of me.

CHAPTER 3

Clark Ranch
Near Ash Fork, Arizona Territory
April 26, 1893

HETTY

"Morning, Mama," I greeted her as I stepped into the dining room with a groggy Remington on my hip. "Papa back yet?"

"No." Mama wrung her hands together. "He should have been back yesterday morning. I'm worried about him."

My nineteen-month-old son chose that moment to kick me as he tried to squirm out of my grip.

"Remi!" I yelled as I tried not to drop him. "Settle down."

"Give food!" he whined.

I set him in his highchair. "Just a minute."

When Rita heard the commotion, she bustled into the dining room with a bowl of cooled oats for him. Then she set it in front of him.

"There you go, niño."

"Juice!" Remi squealed.

I sighed.

"Si. I'll bring you juice," Rita said. Then she came back with the juice, and two biscuits stuffed with eggs and sausage.

"Rio said he saddled your horse. He's outside." She handed me the two biscuits. "One for him."

"Gracias." I gave Mama a peck on the cheek. "I'll head into town to see what is keeping Papa."

"Thank you, sweetheart."

I chomped down on a bite of one biscuit. Then I donned my buckskin fringed jacket and light tan cowboy hat as I rushed out the door.

Some days, like that one, started out with everything going wrong. I overslept, which was entirely unusual for me. Then Remi wouldn't wake up. Thankfully, Rio and Rita Gallegos were used to the inconsistencies of my mornings and planned accordingly.

Rio was the foreman of Clark Ranch for as long as I could remember. He and Papa were close friends before Papa started the ranch. Sometime around when I was seven, Rio met the lovely Rita Chavez. Within the year, they married. Once my childhood cook left the ranch, Rita took over.

They were good people. The sort you could count on for anything. Rita and Mama were both godsends as I tried to raise my son without a father.

"Señorita, no Matthew?"

I shook my head at Rio's question as I handed him the other biscuit. Despite their long friendship, Rio still called Papa by his full name, whereas most of our neighbors and Mama called him Matt.

"Should we go to town first?"

"Depends. You have anything that needs my attention

this morning?" I asked as I mounted my feisty stallion, White Lightning.

"No. Mateo already checked the perimeter. No fresh signs of rustlers today."

"Morning, boy," I whispered as I rubbed my horse's neck. He nodded his head.

Once I turned him toward town, I kicked him into a trot until I finished my breakfast. Then I pushed him for speed, even though there was no urgency. White Lightning was the perfect horse, but only after a brisk morning run.

As we neared the town of Ash Fork, I slowed him to a walk as I gaped at the sight before my eyes. Not a single building stood along the main part of town. Charred remnants of studs poked up from the ground where a four-story hotel once stood. A large tent replaced the burned out saloon at the far end of town.

"What happened?"

"Dios mío," Rio whispered. "Fuego."

Fire. I surveyed the damage as we rode past the crumbled remains of several buildings. In the distance, it surprised me to see the church and parsonage still standing. Two walls of the mercantile next to the church still stood. A smile curled up on one side of my mouth. Seemed God's sense of humor was intact.

Tents lined the streets where buildings once stood. Only a corral remained of the livery.

"Hetty!" a male voice called out to me.

It surprised me he could tell it was me from that distance as I kicked White Lightning into a trot toward the parsonage. I reined him in as Clyde Caldwell jogged toward me.

"Clyde. What happened?"

"Not sure. Two nights ago, fire ripped through the town. Looked like it started near the Blue Diamond."

"You seen Papa?"

Clyde glanced away. "I'm sorry, Hetty."

I dismounted. I was in no mood for ambiguity.

"Clyde, where is he?"

He cleared his throat and nodded to a row of four pine boxes.

The wind left my lungs. I stumbled toward the stairs of the parsonage. I coughed. He couldn't be gone.

"Iris!" He hollered for his wife.

In less than a minute, she sat next to me on the porch stairs. I rubbed my hands on my denim pants as my head pounded. Then I propped my elbows on my legs and dropped my head into my hands.

Clyde cleared his throat. "He ran into a burning building to save a young man."

I snorted and shook my head numbly. "Isn't that just like him?"

"The young man made it out alright. He's staying with us as he recuperates."

"I'm sorry, Hetty," Iris whispered. "When Matt looked for others, the roof collapsed."

Rio walked over to the pine box that Clyde pointed to. He removed his hat and laid a hand on the box.

A lone tear trickled down my cheek. I angrily brushed it away. Ain't no time for crying. I just became the big auger of Clark Ranch. The heaviness of that reality pressed down on my shoulders.

I launched to my feet.

"How do I handle final arrangements?"

"You want to bring your family and men on Friday after-noon for the funeral?"

I nodded. "Let's make it eleven in the morning. That way, I can load up the supplies for the month and head back before nightfall. Are there supplies to be had?"

"Of course," Clyde agreed. "Eleven will be just fine. And yes, there are supplies arriving daily. The Santa Fe, Prescott, & Phoenix Railway is shipping a steady stream of goods into town. So is the Atlantic & Pacific."

"Anything else?" I asked.

"Will you be alright?" Iris asked.

"Yup."

Then I grabbed White Lightning's reins and stomped down the street to a tent where Papa's attorney's office used to exist. I figured Rio would catch up to me later.

"Lucius," I greeted the attorney as I stepped inside the tent.

"Hetty!" He stepped around the crates that held a plank of wood for his makeshift desk. "I'm so sorry. You've heard the news?"

I nodded. "Any chance Papa's will survived?"

"Surprisingly, yes. I pulled out most of my files before the fire reached my building. I put all the paperwork in a wagon and drove it out of town until the fire died out. Though it's not very organized."

"I'm assuming Papa's will names me or Remington as the heir?"

"Give me a few minutes to locate it."

He motioned to an overturned crate. I think he wanted me to sit, but I continued standing. In fact, I paced the length of the tent while he searched for the papers.

"Ah, ha! Here it is."

He sat on the other side of his desk. He flipped through the pages.

"He names you the manager until Remington comes of age. Then it goes to your son."

"Do I have full rights to manage the ranch as I see fit?

Can I buy or sell parcels of land? Purchase new stock?"

Lucius's eyes scanned the document. "Yes. It's as if it belonged to you. The only condition is that it goes to Remington on his eighteenth birthday."

I held out my hand. Lucius shook it. "Thank you. Please get in touch if you discover anything else."

He agreed.

When I stepped out of the tent into the noonday sun, my stomach growled, but I ignored it. Wasn't much point in trying to rustle up some grub in a town stretched thin of resources. Best head back to the ranch.

After I mounted White Lightning, I rode slowly back toward the parsonage. Rio's pinto remained tied to the post. So was my papa's blood bay gelding. My breath snagged at the finality of seeing Papa's unoccupied saddle. Rio stood with his eyes closed and hand on the pine box that contained the empty shell of my papa's body. He wasn't there anymore. No, I knew he was in heaven.

"Hetty?"

My eyes snapped toward the sound of the familiar voice from my dreams. I frowned as recognition dawned. I nudged my horse closer to the parsonage.

"Preston Colter," I spat out his name as if I despised him. My tone contradicted how I really felt about the man. My stupid heartbeat sped up at the sight of those blue eyes. He made all rational thought flee from my mind. I kept my face stoic, as I hoped he wouldn't see how he affected me after all those years.

"I'm sorry for your loss."

I supposed I should get used to folks expressing condolences. I should know how to respond. Only I didn't. Not a grunt. Not a thanks. Not a nod of my head.

I cleared my throat.

"How you holding up?"

My heart cracked at the sincere concern in his voice. I couldn't let it in. Not if I hoped to survive the coming days and weeks. My mama and my son needed me to be strong, like Papa always was. I became the head of the family.

"You look..." My words faded as my thoughts rolled through my observations. He looked rough. Unshaven. Barely sober. Dirty. About the same as the last time I saw him over two and a half years ago.

I finally settled on what I ought to say. "Well."

He glanced away.

I snorted and turned my horse away from him.

"Rio!"

My foreman stirred and mounted his pinto. I kicked my horse forward out of town.

If that didn't beat all. After years of wondering what had happened to Preston Colter, he stood before me. I swore he read my mind. Heard my condescending thoughts.

Well, good for him. It wouldn't hurt for him to know we weren't exactly on speaking terms. Not after he left me without a word. Disappeared to who knew where. Even if I had wanted to force him to marry me and give my son a respectable life, I couldn't. Hadn't seen hide nor hare of the man since December 1890.

The dark circles under his eyes betrayed his sleepless nights. His wrinkled shirt needed a good scrubbing. If I read the signs right, he was a little over thirty-six hours sober. I didn't need a lushington in my life. Not again. No matter how handsome he was or how he made my heart skip a beat or three.

No, Remi and I were better off without the bandido.

CHAPTER 4

PRESTON

When I stepped out of the Caldwell's home to find the outhouse, my breath left me. I rubbed my eyes.

"Hetty?"

It was her. She sat atop a white stallion with her light tan cowboy hat pulled low. She wore a blue plaid shirt under a buckskin jacket with long fringes lining the sleeves.

Even from my vantage point, I could see her frown.

Then she said my name with vitriol. I supposed I deserved it. The last time I saw her, we made love. Then I disappeared the next morning with no word about where I was going. Not once since then did I send her a note or a letter or give her any indication as to my whereabouts. At that moment, I realized it had been a mistake.

Clyde told me at breakfast that Matt Clark, her father, was the man who saved my life. I still found that bit of news difficult to chew over. The man was a saint. He sacrificed his life to save a lowlife like me. Surely, he recognized it was me when he pulled me from the burning building.

"I'm sorry for your loss." More than I could convey right then.

I sensed her eyes studying me, though her hat shaded them too much for me to know for certain.

"How you holding up?" I asked. I really cared. Far more than I wanted to admit.

"You look…"

At her lengthy pause, I assessed what she truly thought. I looked unkempt. Hungover. Filthy. Not someone she'd want to talk to.

"Well."

I nodded.

Before I knew it, she turned, called for her foreman, and rode out of town. I watched her ride away. Smooth and confident in the saddle. I shook my head. Of course, her horse was a stallion. Only woman with enough gumption to ride a horse like that. And her beauty still surpassed all other women in the territory.

I continued on to the outhouse before I returned to the Caldwell's.

"When's the funeral?" I asked when I entered the house.

Clyde frowned. "Friday. Why?"

"I know Hetty. The least I can do is pay my respects to the man who saved my life."

"Don't think that's a good idea," Iris said as she poured me a coffee. "Didn't sound like she was pleased to see you."

As I sipped coffee, I said nothing more. I would keep to the shadows and the background. I was plenty good at that.

My head pounded and my hand shook as I tried to raise the cup to my lips. It was starting. Beads of sweat dotted my forehead and dripped down the side of my face.

"You ought to go lie down," Clyde said.

As I set the coffee cup down, my hand shook so violently that I dropped it, spilling the hot liquid on my hand and shirt sleeve. I cursed. Then I apologized to Iris as she stood and grabbed my arm. She dragged me to the sink and ran cool water over the burn.

My legs shook, and it took an enormous amount of effort to stay upright. I gripped the edge of the sink so hard my knuckles turned white.

"Clyde," Iris called her husband over.

He looped an arm around my waist and helped me back to the bed in their guest room. By the time we made it there, my mind grew fuzzy and tremors overtook my entire body. Not soon enough for me, I passed out.

———

Over the next few days, I was boogered up. Hallucinations consumed my mind. The withdrawals were significantly worse than last time.

Iris and Clyde took turns sitting with me. They brought cool cloths for my face. I eventually stripped down to my underthings and still ended up drenched.

One time, during a violent episode, I caught Clyde praying for me. I didn't know why the man and his wife bothered with me. I didn't deserve an ounce of kindness. Yet, they gave me more than just kindness. They were truly concerned about my wellbeing.

Finally, early Friday morning, before the sun rose, the tremors lessened, and the fever subsided. My mind cleared.

I ventured into their washroom. After I drew myself a cold bath, I scrubbed every square inch of my filthy body. I didn't bother trying to figure out how to shave. Instead, I scrubbed my beard and hair clean.

By the time I finished, the smell of breakfast wafted down the hall. When I opened the door, a clean pair of denim pants, underthings, and a plaid shirt sat on the floor. I snagged them and closed the washroom door to change into clean clothes.

I made my way to the kitchen.

"Morning," Clyde greeted me.

"Thank you, Iris, for the fresh change of clothes."

"You're quite welcome," she said as she smiled and set a plate of food in front of me.

I bowed my head, as I knew their tradition of blessing the food. When Clyde finished, I picked up my fork. My hand shook, though not so badly that I couldn't eat.

"You still having your meeting?" Iris asked. "With two funerals today, is there time?"

"The posse will be here around noon. Hope it won't be too much trouble to fix lunch today with everything else going on?"

"Not at all. I'll start cooking a hearty stew after breakfast."

"You gonna join us?" Clyde asked.

I blinked. "On a posse? Not sure I'm well enough to ride."

Clyde laughed. "It's not a real posse. That's just what I call our little group of ex-drunks."

I straightened my back and glanced down the side of my nose. I figured the Caldwells had some sort of plan for me when they took me in.

I cleared my throat.

"Have lunch with us and see what you think," Clyde said. "No pressure."

Didn't see the point in meeting a bunch of former drunks. Wasn't sure I wanted to be one myself.

"Alright," I said even though I didn't want to.

As soon as I finished my breakfast, I headed out of the house. The thought of sticking around for the ex-drunk lunch made my skin crawl. Besides, I was past due searching for my horse and hoped that no one stole Ranger or sold him.

I walked over to the large makeshift corral where all the unidentified horses had been gathered. One of the livery owners in town took care of them.

"Morning," I said as I ambled toward a man with black hair and a long, stringy mustache.

"Morning," he greeted me. "Name's Rich Bollinger. How can I help you?"

Once I introduced myself, I said, "I was wondering if you've seen a liver chestnut stallion? I left him near the Blue Diamond the night of the fire."

"I think I've got one unclaimed. What's his name?"

"Ranger. Should have a medium brown saddle with redd-ish undertones. Initials P.C. towards the front."

"Come on back," Rich offered.

I walked into the corral and studied the lighter colored horses. None of them wore saddles. As I moved through the corral, several horses came up to me. I figured they knew a wrangler when they saw one. I rubbed their noses for a minute before I walked to the next.

"Got a gift with horses, huh?"

"Yup."

Then I saw him. Ranger stood off to the side. Wasn't that just like him? As much of an outcast as me. I whistled, and his ears perked up. He snorted and wandered over to me. He nickered at me and nudged my arm with his muzzle.

"Miss me?"

He sighed as I rubbed his forehead.

Rich chuckled. "I'd say that's a yes."

"How much it cost to board him for a few more days?" I

asked.

He named the price, and I frowned. I was hard pushed. Didn't have enough to pay for more than a day or two.

"You know," Rich said, "I could use some help caring for the horses if you're available."

"I got somewhere to be this morning, but I could help this afternoon."

I didn't want to over-commit. Especially since I didn't know how much longer I'd stay there. I needed a new job, and I was running out of ranches that would hire me. Clark and Bartholomew were about the only places I hadn't worked, and I doubted Hetty would hire me. Not after her cold greeting the other day.

"We can play it by ear. You can work in exchange for board and feed for Ranger."

Rich led the way as I followed him back into the tent where he stored the tack for the horses he took in. When I found my saddle, I was relieved. Didn't have money to replace it.

After I thanked Rich, I headed back over to Caldwell's. It must have been later than I expected. I recognized Hetty's stallion tied to the post. A middle-aged woman stepped down from a carriage. As I ducked behind the edge of the house, I heard the squeals of a toddler. The woman called after him.

Poor woman. There had to be nearly twenty years between the toddler and Hetty. It was a bigger gap than my oldest brother, James, and my younger sister, Vi. I shook my head.

I watched from the side of the house. Hetty held out her arms for her brother. He giggled and jumped into her arms.

Something tugged at my heart at the sight. She was good with him. That thought brought me something I almost never felt: happiness.

When they headed toward the cemetery, I followed at a distance. I took Iris's warning seriously and made sure my presence went unnoticed.

Five cowboys, the foreman, and a Mexican woman joined Hetty, her brother, and her mother, Tildy, if I remembered her name. A few minutes later, other ranchers and men from the community filled the graveyard. I moved back as more people arrived.

Clyde and Iris stood at the front. He held a Bible. Then he led the service, and it finally dawned on me that Clyde was a pastor. Don't know why I hadn't figured it out before then.

I listened as Clyde read a passage that seemed confusing to me.

"For in this tent, we groan, longing to put on our heavenly dwelling... For while we are still in this tent, we groan, being burdened—not that we would be unclothed, but that we would be further clothed, so that what is mortal may be swallowed up by life."

I leaned forward, hoping he might explain it.

"You see, Paul is talking about the journey that Matt has gone on. He was in this tent or body a few days ago. Now he has put on his heavenly dwelling, further clothed. In what? His good deeds on earth? No, Matt's good deeds poured out of him because of his love for God. He didn't do good deeds to earn some standing with God. He already had that standing because he believed that what this book says is true—that Jesus sacrificed himself to make a way for Matt, for me, and," he looked directly at me, "for you."

I swallowed the lump in my throat. My heart raced.

"Even the worst among us can choose to accept that. When we do, we don't have to feel sorrowful about death.

We can look forward to a new life, a new body in heaven that Jesus prepared for us."

Clyde cleared his throat. "So today, even though we are sad to say goodbye to what was mortal, Matt's life on earth, we can celebrate his new home and new life in heaven."

"In that same passage, Paul says that the old has passed away, and the new has come. He tells us that our old sinful self is no longer counted against us, but Jesus's sacrifice reconciled us and made us new."

My eyes burned as the words penetrated my heart. Matt sacrificed himself to save my worthless life. It was such a tangible parallel to the sacrifice of Jesus that Clyde described.

I knew about the Bible. Some stories about men of renown. I knew about Jesus. But I didn't truly understand the depth of what it meant. Not until that moment.

I wasn't ready to face it and what it meant for me or my life. When I turned on my heel, I ran headlong into Rich.

"Preston."

I looked away. I wanted to run away. Run to the saloon. Run from everything stirring inside of me.

"You coming in for lunch?"

CHAPTER 5

HETTY

Two days did little to improve Mama's grief. My heart shredded as I thought back to her piercing wails when I returned home with Papa's empty saddle. The pain in her eyes. I couldn't describe it.

My parents shared a deep bond. One that I thought I might not get to experience myself. I had no way to understand Mama's heartache. Even Remi getting hurt seemed insignificant compared to what haunted her.

It took a great deal of intention to keep my emotions at bay. As I stood at Papa's graveside, I wanted to fall to my knees. I wanted to scream and wail and beat my fists against the ground.

Instead, I pasted a stoic expression on my face. I pretended I had no heart left in which to squeeze an ounce of feeling from. I had to be strong for Mama. For Remi. Perhaps even a little for myself.

When Mama grabbed my arm tighter and her sniffles turned to sobs, I barely held it together. I glanced off into the distance.

Clyde's words felt comforting. Picturing Papa in heaven

as a young man in a new body brought me solace. Bright smile. Walking next to Jesus in his heavenly dwelling.

I coughed to hide the sob rising in my throat. Too many people depended on me to be strong. To be the rock.

But inside, I felt a lot more like quicksand. I was sinking fast. And I couldn't sink. If I did, the entire family would. Rio and Rita. The cowboys. They needed a powerful leader. A fearless warrior.

I possessed strength and grit in spades. I tamed wild horses. My ornery stallion submitted to my lead. I raised my son without his father. I was strong.

My nails dug into my palm as I fisted my hand. I must keep my composure at the funeral. Just a few more minutes. Then I would ask Mama to watch Remi, and I would ride home by myself. I'd find some place to fall apart in private—to give in to the sorrow cutting through my heart.

When I thought I could not stand it a moment longer, I handed Remi to Mama. Then I turned around.

My heart lodged in my throat. My stomach tightened. The crowd behind me overwhelmed me. At least forty people attended, besides those of us from the ranch.

My eyes burned. I bit the inside of my cheek and lifted my chin as I straightened my back. Then I walked through the crowd.

They took off their hats and said nothing as I passed by them.

One tear. Then two.

By the time I made it to the back of the crowd and onto White Lightning, my tears flowed freely. I squeezed my stallion's sides, and he lurched into a gallop.

As soon as I was out of town, I pulled him up and dismounted. Then my legs buckled beneath me. I held on to his reins as I collapsed to the ground.

So many questions ran through my mind. Why did God take him home now? Why was I left alone? Could I be as strong as I must?

I missed Papa. His hearty laughter. His frequent smile. His teasing. His unending support of me and my ambitions. His unfathomable love and forgiveness.

I still remembered when I told him about my pregnancy. It was the hardest thing I ever did. Yet, he showed me love through that entire conversation, despite his disappointment.

Instead, he encouraged me. He promised he and Mama would help. Papa made sure Remi and I would never want for anything. In return, I threw my entire being into becoming the best rancher I could. I vowed never to disappoint him again.

Now my rock, my papa, was gone. Remi would grow up without a father or a grandfather.

"Papa, we both need you. Why did you save a stranger from a burning building?"

I shook my head. I knew why he did it. He always did things like that because he lived out his faith. He was a better person than I could ever hope to be.

I swiped the back of my hand across my eyes. Then I stood and mounted White Lightning and headed home.

———

PRESTON

Rich wouldn't let me pass. It was like he could read the thoughts running through my head. Like he knew how it felt.

Another man stood next to us as the crowd from the funeral thinned out.

"Afternoon, Brian," Rich said before he introduced me.

I felt trapped between Brian Turner and Rich, so I just followed them into the Caldwell's home. The smell of stew permeated the house. I had eaten almost nothing for a few days and the smell made my stomach growl.

A third man entered the house and introduced himself as Thomas Erwin. Rich dished up five bowls of the stew and set them on the table.

Seemed presumptuous to me to help himself.

When Clyde entered the kitchen, he smiled.

"I see you met our guest."

"Oh, I met him this morning at the livery. Reunited him with his horse," Rich said.

Iris entered the kitchen and dished up a bowl for herself. Then she took it to the porch.

"Brian, you want to say grace?" Clyde asked.

Brian nodded and bowed his head. He thanked God for the newcomer at the table. I frowned. I wasn't someone to be thankful for.

"Amen," Clyde said, drawing my thoughts back to the table.

As we ate, I listened to Brian talk about his work at the saddlery. Thomas was the railroad station manager. Rich asked how their week had been.

"Alright. The temptation gets less and less as time goes by," Thomas admitted.

"So the additional days haven't been too hard?" Clyde asked.

"No. Far too busy with the influx of activity at the station."

"We usually meet on Wednesday afternoon," Rich said

to me.

I nodded, still unclear why I was there.

"How long has it been?" Brian asked.

"Seventeen months," Thomas said.

"I hope I make it that long," Brian admitted.

"You know we don't hope in our own strength," Clyde reminded him.

I swallowed a bite of the stew. "How long has it been?"

"Nine months for me. Rich has three years and Clyde ten."

I blinked. "For what?"

"Since our last drink," Clyde said.

I rubbed my temples. I forgot he said the ex-drunks were coming for lunch. My brain was still foggy from the withdrawal.

"And you?" Rich asked.

After I cleared my throat, I said, "I suppose four days now."

"Ah, so this is the first you've had an appetite?" Brian asked.

"I suppose."

Clyde smiled. "He's only picked at his food. Looks like he's hungry now."

As they talked about daily life, I felt less awkward. They seemed like nice enough men. Their ages varied widely. Clyde was in his fifties. Rich was in his late thirties. Thomas was maybe in his early thirties. Brian was between my age and Thomas.

They talked for about an hour before Thomas stood and started water in the sink. Brian dried dishes while Thomas washed them.

"Preston, would you mind fetching my wife's bowl?" Clyde asked.

I stood and walked out onto the porch. Iris smiled when she saw me.

"Friendly group of men, aren't they?"

"I… I suppose."

"It seems God keeps sending men like them across our path. These meetings that Clyde organized really helps them stay strong and committed to living alcohol-free."

Didn't plan to be among their number. I had no issue with drinking. It was the withdrawals that made it so unbearable.

"I guess you probably came out here for this," she said as she handed me the empty bowl. "Thank you so much."

When I took it, I started to leave. Then I stopped and faced her again.

"Why would you thank me? Why do you and Clyde bother with a scoundrel like me? I ain't a good man. I don't even think I want to stop drinking."

She smiled. "You are here, aren't you?"

I blinked. She said nothing more, as if her words explained everything.

"I best get this inside. Since he's boarding Ranger, I promised Rich I'd help care for the horses at the livery."

"Thanks again!" she called after me.

I walked back to the kitchen and gave the bowl to Thomas.

"What is it you do, Preston?" Brian asked.

I snorted. "I'm between jobs at the moment."

"Of course you are," Thomas said. "When you are working, what do you like to do?"

I frowned as the nosy questions made the hair on the back of my neck stand on end.

"Seems you have a gift with horses," Rich said. "It was obvious when you came by the livery this morning. If I'd guess, I'd say you're a wrangler."

"Oh, wasn't Matt Clark looking for a wrangler?" Brian asked.

Clyde nodded. "Yup. Last one just up and quit a few weeks ago. I figure with Hetty taking over the ranch, she'll need one even more."

"Why's that?" I asked, trying to be friendly. A part of me wouldn't mind working at her ranch. But I really wanted to run far away again.

"Before her son was born, she used to fill in when they were between wranglers. Between her little boy and taking over the ranch, I doubt she'll have the time."

Clyde's words left me as winded as when I fell off a bronco landing on my back. The little boy wasn't Hetty's brother. He was her son. I gripped the back of the closest chair as my heart raced.

"Where's the boy's father?" Brian asked, sparing me from saying the words.

Clyde's gaze pinned me. "Don't know. She never said."

"Well," Rich said as he squeezed my shoulder, "If you're feeling up to it, I could use your help at the livery. Best be heading back."

We said our farewells. Then I followed him to his temporary livery. After he showed me around, I helped him set up a few makeshift stalls, where I took the horses to brush them down one by one. Even though I still felt some after-effects of the liquor sickness, the work soothed me. My hands shook, but I still did the job.

Working with horses was what I loved to do. It was just dealing with people that seemed to trigger the feelings that I wanted to escape from.

"You know," Rich said as he brushed down a horse in the stall next to me. "Maybe you should head out to the

Clark's ranch on Monday. I'm guessing the tremors should settle by then."

"I don't know that Hetty would have any interest in hiring me."

"Why not? You're clearly great with horses."

"We have history."

"Ah." Rich nodded his head.

When he turned the horse loose in the corral and brought another one back, he pressed it again.

"Still, she's gonna need the help, and you've got the skills. You need a job and a roof over your head if you hope to stay sober."

"What do you know about it?" I growled.

"I know that the longer a man stays idle, the more likely he is to turn back to his vices, whatever they may be. Clyde and Iris are soft on the fellas they take in. I sense soft ain't what's gonna motivate you to move on."

After I finished brushing down the gray mare, I led her back to the corral. Then I brought back a palomino.

"I was thinking I might head back to my family's ranch in Prescott."

Rich snorted. "You that afraid to confront your history with Hetty?"

My hand stilled as I straightened to look at Rich over the horse's back. The man had some determination. Unfortunately, it was rubbing me the wrong way.

He smiled. "If you think family is what you need right now, then by all means, save up for a train ticket and head on home."

I grunted and returned to caring for the palomino. I could only imagine what would happen if I showed up at Colter Ranch. Mama would coddle me. I doubted Sam would hire me on. Only if Papa forced him to. And I wasn't too sure Papa would.

Besides, going home felt too much like admitting defeat. I knew they would never leave me destitute. And I'd have to face all the feelings I kept trying to run from.

Maybe Rich was right. Maybe I should take a chance that Hetty might hire me. Seemed like my best option as I tried to start over again.

CHAPTER 6

HETTY

By the time Monday rolled around, I felt stronger. Besides the ride home after the funeral, I took another long ride yesterday morning to set my mind right. I said goodbye to Papa. I would still miss him, like at mealtimes when his chair remained vacant. But I was prepared to run the ranch.

I sat at his desk reviewing the ledger mid-morning when Mav hurried into the house.

"Rider coming," he said.

I set the ledgers aside. "Is it John?"

"Not sure. Don't recognize the horse."

"Alright. If you don't mind, escort our visitor to the front porch. I'll be out in a minute."

Mav nodded and left.

I straightened my back. It would make sense if John Bartholomew showed up. I knew Papa discussed the possibility of selling a section of our land to him. The parcel bordered Bartholomew Ranch. When the railroad came through, it cut off that section from our main grazing lands, so that land didn't benefit us anymore. Made more sense for John and his brother, Jacob, to own it.

As I walked to the door, I peered out the window. Mav was right. The rider was too young and thin to be John. Plus, John rode a black gelding, not a liver chestnut horse.

I fastened my gun belt around my hips. One could never be too careful when a stranger showed up unexpectedly. Especially since word would have gotten out that the house was full of a bunch of unprotected women. A stranger would not know I was as much of a threat as any man if the situation called for it.

After I donned my hat, I opened the door and stepped onto the porch. The moment I did, I recognized the rider.

"Preston Colter. What is he doing here?" I said under my breath.

"You know him, boss?" Mav asked.

I snorted.

"You want me to stick around?"

"No. He's no threat. I'll see what he wants and send him on his way."

"I won't go too far. Just holler if you change your mind."

My pulse raced as Preston dismounted his horse. He stood at the bottom of the porch, looking ridiculously handsome. His freshly shaved face revealed his angled jawline and powerful neck. When he took off his hat, the sun glinted in those incredible blue eyes. Gone were the dark circles under them.

"Why are you here?" I spat out the words as I tried to regain control of my senses.

"May I come in?"

"We can converse on the porch just fine."

When he joined me on the porch, I stepped back a few paces, giving him a wide berth.

Preston cleared his throat as he gripped his hat tightly.

"I heard you need a wrangler."

I narrowed my eyes.

"I think you already know I'm quite good with horses. Thought I'd stop by to see if you could use my help."

Though his voice sounded humble, his words triggered my ire.

"Your help. That's ironic."

He said nothing as I crossed my arms. Then I uncrossed them and stepped closer to him. I jabbed my finger in his chest.

"Two and a half years ago, you whispered charming words of love to me, coaxed me into your bed for a few nights, then you up and left. Is that the help you think I need?"

His gaze darted to the floor.

I propped my hands on my hips. "You left me. You disappeared without a trace."

"I..."

I paced the length of the porch, trying to calm down. My anger was even hotter than I expected.

"Do you know how much that hurt? For months, Papa and I tried to find you. Figure out where you went. We came up empty."

"I'm sorry."

As I turned to walk back toward him, I halted. The anguish written on his face shocked me. It was so unexpected that my tirade died on the tip of my tongue.

"What I did, Hetty, I have no excuse for it. I was selfish. I was wrong. I know I hurt you. And all I can say is I'm sorry."

As I leaned against the side of the house, I blew out a loud breath.

"Mav!" I yelled.

He arrived in a few seconds. "Yes, boss."

"Show our new wrangler to his bunk and introduce him to the horses."

"Sure thing."

Preston followed him, but then stopped and called over his shoulder. "Thank you, Hetty."

I growled and yanked the door of the house open. Once I stepped through, I slammed it shut before I strode into my office.

What possessed me, I did not know. It was foolish to hire him. Foolish to let him live so near.

Maybe being like my papa wasn't a good thing. He always took in every stray man or beast. Gave people second chances. Always hoped for the best. I was his daughter, and I learned those lessons well.

Only Preston wasn't a stray or a stranger. He was the father of my son, and he still held some fascinating grip on my heart.

But his face. His eyes were clear. His appearance led me to believe he was sober. For how long, only time would tell. And his apology seemed sincere.

"Hetty?" Mama called my name as she entered the office. "Something troubling you?"

I threw my hands up in the air and let them fall to my sides. "I just hired a new wrangler is all."

"You seem a bit upset about that."

"I'll be fine."

It was silly not to tell her immediately that I had hired Preston. She would find out soon enough.

Later that afternoon, after I calmed down considerably, I headed out to the barn. I found Preston reorganizing the tack room. When I stepped into the room, he held my father's saddle.

"What are you doing with that?" I asked.

"I was just moving some things around."

My eyes burned and I willed my emotions away.

"I know it was your father's. Let's place it over here, so I remember to polish it regularly. I'm guessing you're keeping it for your son?"

Had he stabbed a knife directly into my heart, it would have hurt less. His intuition was dead on.

Words failed me, so I settled for a nod. I watched as he carefully placed Papa's saddle by itself on a special stand. Then he rubbed a hand along the smooth leather.

"I will take care of it, Hetty."

I glanced away.

"I'm sure that's not what brought you out here, though."

I cleared my throat and straightened my back. "No, it's not."

The fire I felt as I walked to the barn earlier vanished. I pulled a stool over and sat on it. I motioned for him to sit on another.

"I wanted to set some rules."

He nodded and crossed his arms over his lean chest.

"Don't forget that I know you, Preston."

He glanced away.

After I took a deep breath, I kept my voice steady, like I had seen Papa do with the strays he took in.

"There is no drinking on my property. Not a drop. If the boys offer you some, you decline it. While you work for me, when you go into town, you don't go to the saloon. You don't find some buddies to sneak liquor to you."

His eyes snapped back to mine.

"As long as you stay dry, you can have this job. But if I catch even a hint of you sneaking around drinking, I will not hesitate to drag your sorry behind into town and leave you there to rot."

"Understood."

I smiled. "Good."

As I stood, I motioned for him to follow me. "Now, I will need your help training."

"Pardon?"

I turned to face him and my breath caught. He was closer than I expected.

"I… I'm entering the cowboy tournament this year. I'm a little rusty, with 1890 being my last competition, so I need you to help get me into bronco riding shape."

He snorted. "Do you really think that's wise?"

"Well, that's an odd question coming from you."

"What if you get hurt?"

I laughed. "'Course, I'm gonna get hurt. It's a bronco."

He grabbed my arms, and lightning shot up them straight to my heart.

"I'm serious. If something happens to you…" He coughed. "Who would take care of your mother and your son?"

I pulled my arms from his grip and backed up a few steps.

"Nothing is going to happen to me. You remember I won first-place two years in a row?"

He leaned up against the stable wall and crossed one leg in front of the other.

"Yeah, well, that was three years ago. Two months isn't enough time to get ready, especially after such a long break."

"I'm not changing my mind about this. And I just hired myself a new wrangler. A wrangler whose job it is to take care of my horses, clean the stables, manage the tack, and help me prepare for the competition. You got a problem with that?"

Preston narrowed his blue eyes. "No, ma'am."

"Good. We start first thing tomorrow morning."

Then I turned and strode out of the barn, grumbling to myself. He had some nerve standing up to me. He was on my ranch, working for me. If I wanted to enter the competition, I could enter it.

At supper that night, I mentioned it to Mama.

"What do you mean, you are competing again?" She glanced at Remi. "Do you really think that's wise?"

I groaned. "Why does everyone act like I've got a screw loose?"

Mama narrowed her eyes.

"I have not gone off my nut. May I remind you I competed and won two years in a row?"

"Yes, well. You didn't have a family of your own."

I let her have the last word at supper, even as I resolved to pursue practicing for the competition, anyway. Even though I hadn't ridden a bronc in a few years, I could do it again and place.

Besides, I needed something to look forward to if I had any hope of moving past Papa's death without completely falling apart.

CHAPTER 7

PRESTON

That first night at Hetty's ranch was harder than I expected. She gave me the reason I needed to quit drinking. If I wanted to be around her, I must stay sober.

When I entered the bunkhouse that night, several of the cowboys enjoyed a drink while they played cards. When I declined to be social, the loneliness hit me hard. I unpacked my meager belongings on my designated shelf. Then I took my pouch of tobacco and cigarette papers and headed outside, figuring I stood a better chance of not drinking if I wasn't around it.

I rolled myself a few cigarettes and put them in my case. Then I lit one. As I leaned against the bunkhouse, I took a long drag before I slowly blew out the smoke.

As I considered the events of the last week, I hardly believed that I had nearly died. Hetty's father saved me. I got sober, found Hetty again, and got a decent job. Seemed like a lot to take in. And the posse in town were men I thought I could call friends. They went out of their way to include me in their group.

Tomorrow seemed far away as I fought against the intense pull of the drink. When I finished my cigarette, I stuffed my hands in my pockets and walked toward the barn. Sure, I spent the better part of the day there. But it was the only place I thought would distract me.

When I pushed open the door, I stopped in my tracks. Hetty crouched next to her little boy. Her long blond hair was loose and hung down to her waist. She smiled as he laughed. I couldn't hear what she whispered to him. Whatever it was caused him to squeal and raise his arms. She picked him up and opened the gate on the stall in front of them.

It was wrong to invade their private moment, but I moved closer to the stall. It was next to Ranger's, which was where I intended to go, so I ambled that direction.

"Horsey!" her son exclaimed and giggled. "Ride horsey!"

I glanced in the stall, planning to continue on to the next one. When I saw the pure joy on the boy's face, I froze. Such innocence. No pain. No fear. No darkness. He was sweet and happy and amazing. His blue eyes sparkled with delight. His dark hair stood on end.

Without realizing it, I smiled.

"Pop Pop!"

A lump formed in my throat.

Hetty's posture stiffened. She cleared her throat.

"I'm sorry, Remi. Pop Pop is with Jesus now."

Then he pointed at me. "Pop Pop!"

She followed his extended arm until her gaze rested on me.

"Evening," I greeted her.

A shadow fell over her face. Then she turned her attention to Remi.

"That's the new horse man. Preston."

Remi giggled. "Horse man!"

I laughed. "I suppose I've been called worse things."

She snorted. Then she held out her arms for him. He slid into her hold before she turned toward me.

"Remi, this is Preston. Preston, this is Remington Clark. He doesn't know it yet, but he owns this whole ranch."

Her green eyes connected with mine as she pressed her lips into a thin line.

"Hello, Remington." I extended my hand. "I'm your new horse man."

He grabbed my finger and giggled. "Horse man!"

I smiled and my heart warmed.

"I'm surprised you're in here. I thought you finished for the day."

As I wiggled my finger, Remi kept hold of it. I made a few funny faces, which earned me a smile.

"I was. Came to check on Ranger. I was thinking about a ride."

"Sun's already set. I wouldn't recommend it."

"Hadn't thought it through all the way." I slowly pulled my finger away from Remi.

"I'm surprised you aren't hanging out with the boys."

As I looked away under her fierce gaze, I cleared my throat. "They were playing cards and such."

"Ah."

Her tone told me she understood my meaning.

"Good to see you chose a smarter path."

I looked at her then. The soft glow of the lantern hanging in the stall made her hair shine. Her eyes looked sad. Her features relaxed and her sweet lips almost curled into a smile, but not quite.

I stood there studying her for far too long. Her eyes

traveled over my face as well. Had her son not been there, I would have tried to kiss her. That would have been a mistake. A disastrous mistake. She was my boss now. A wrong step with her would be the end.

She cleared her throat. "If you don't mind." She nodded toward the gate. "This little one needs to go to bed for the night."

I opened the gate and stepped aside, keeping it between her and me, lest I caved to the temptation to pull her into my arms.

"Good night, Preston."

"Horse man!"

I laughed. "Good night, all."

Just like that, she and Remi disappeared, taking the light with them. I stood in the dark, watching as they walked back to the house.

What an idiot I had been to leave her. She was perfect in every way. Even the perfect mother. A niggling feeling tried to sneak into my heart. I wondered who his father was. And I almost wondered if it was me.

As soon as the thought came, I shook it off. Didn't really matter. He was her son. Wore the Clark name. Clearly, it was exactly as she wanted it.

I returned to the barn and Ranger's stall. I rubbed his nose and murmured to him for a while before I retired to the bunkhouse for the night.

The next morning, I woke at the first sound of activity in the bunkhouse. A few of the cowboys bemoaned daylight. I figured they were the ones who stayed up long past when I retired. I greeted each of them as I took a seat at the table.

Rita entered the building, with Rio following behind. While she cooked some grub, he took a seat at the table.

"Boss wants us to limit the alcohol consumption to the weekends," Rio said. "Friday night and Saturday only."

Landry and Austin whined, but Rio gave them a steely look, and they clammed up.

I frowned, pretty sure the new rule was intended to help me. I didn't want special treatment.

"She also wants us to keep the herd in the north pasture for a few days. She's concerned about rustlers trying to take advantage of a ranch run by a señorita."

"Colter, she wants you in the corral with the bronco immediately following breakfast. The boys typically saddle their own mounts in the morning, anyway."

I nodded and thanked Rita as she set the first plate of bacon and eggs in front of me. She also placed a plate of biscuits in the center of the table. I scarfed down the food as I wanted a few minutes with the bronco.

As soon as I finished, I excused myself and hurried to the barn. I found the feistiest horse and figured that was the bronco. He seemed like more than a handful. Once I got him ready, I led him to the practice chute.

My stomach tightened as Hetty approached. Her hair was braided, and she wore denim pants under her chaps. Leather gloves fit tightly over her slender hands.

"He's pretty wild. You sure you want to do this?" I asked as she approached.

She narrowed her eyes. Then she climbed over the side of the fence and sat on the back of the horse. He snorted and fussed the second her rear connected with his back.

"Maybe we should get one of the boys to help."

"Ready," she said.

I sighed and flipped the gate open.

The horse instantly lunged forward on his front legs. After clearing the gate, he pushed up his hindquarters, then reared up. Hetty almost immediately lost her grip and top-pled over his back end. She landed hard on her backside.

"Oof."

I dashed toward the wild animal and grabbed his reins. Once I controlled the horse, I glanced over to where she sat in the dirt. The frown on her forehead and the set of her jaw told me she was determined to try again.

"You looking for any observations?" I asked.

"If I want your opinion, I'll ask."

I shrugged and led the horse back into the chute.

She climbed up on his back again with very similar results.

After the third attempt, she growled. "Fine. What do you think?"

"You're timing is off. He's controlling your motion. Instead, you need to control your motion when you lean forward and when you lean back. You're riding like a tenderfoot."

She frowned at me. "Let's see you try."

"I ain't been on a bronco in a year."

"Well, that's more recent than me. Show me how it's done."

I narrowed my eyes at her. I knew her well enough to know that I had one choice, and it was to uncork the bronc. Doubted how I'd fare. I was barely over the alcohol sickness. Certainly not in any shape to ride a bronco.

"Here." I thrust the reins toward her.

I hopped on the back of the crazy horse. Then I leaned forward slightly, anticipating he'd exit the chute the same way he had on his other runs.

When I nodded, Hetty opened the chute.

Sure enough, he started downward. I leaned back just before he kicked up his back legs. Then I leaned forward as he reared up. I stayed on for a few seconds as I discerned his movements. Once I chewed gravel, Hetty grabbed his reins.

"Something like that," I said as I brushed the dirt from my hat. "Now you try."

She climbed up on his back. Just like I did, she started with a slight lean forward. Then she anticipated his movements. She stayed on for about four seconds. Best time so far, but not remotely close to competition worthy.

Hetty insisted on four more runs before I suggested we call it a day. She was about to climb onto his back again when I spotted riders in the distance.

"Expecting visitors?"

Her gaze followed the direction I nodded. "No."

"That's probably enough for today."

She grunted. Then she jumped down and headed toward the barn where she retrieved her gun belt.

"As soon as you put him away, can you keep an eye out?" she asked.

"Yes ma'am."

As she headed back to the house, I quickly cared for the bronco. Then I fastened on my gun belt and headed toward the house. The riders pulled to a stop right as I arrived.

"Afternoon, Hetty," the older gentleman on the black gelding said. "I've come with a proposal."

My heart lodged in my throat as I hoped the proposal was business and not a romantic one.

"John. Jacob. Come on in. I'm sure Mama will be happy about your visit."

When I stepped onto the porch, she turned to me. "Can you see to their horses?"

"You can turn them out in the corral," the other man said. "We won't make a nuisance by staying too long."

I nodded and led the horses to the corral. As I let them

loose, I watched as the two men disappeared into the house behind Hetty, wondering what business they had with her.

CHAPTER 8

HETTY

"Mama, we have visitors," I called out as I entered the house.

Mama breezed into the main room and smiled when she recognized our neighbors, the Bartholomew brothers.

"John, Jacob, what a delightful surprise. Can I fetch you some coffee and pie?"

Jacob grinned. "That would be a treat."

"Come, have a seat at the table."

"We're sorry for your loss," John said as he set his hat aside.

"Thank you." Mama sniffed and hurried into the kitchen.

"And yours as well," John said, as he took my hand in his.

I removed my hand from his and stuffed it in my pocket. "Much appreciated."

Then I took a seat at the table across from him and his brother.

"I suppose you are wondering if we still want to sell the parcel you and Papa discussed."

"Well, yes, and no." John thanked Mama as she set coffee and pie in front of him. "Jacob and I were thinking, considering your loss, that another plan might be amenable."

He glanced at me before he took a gulp of his coffee. He seemed nervous.

Jacob picked up the conversation. "We were thinking with your father's untimely passing that you could use a man to run the ranch."

I sipped my coffee and straightened in my chair.

"I had broached the idea with your father back when…" John coughed. "Right before your son was born."

My heart raced as I hoped I was very wrong about John's intentions. He was roughly ten years older than my parents. I held back the urge to shiver.

"What I'm suggesting… It would be a matter of convenience for you. I wouldn't ask you for normal marital privileges."

When he finally voiced the idea, I nearly choked on my coffee.

"Marriage?!" I shrieked. "What makes you think I'm look-ing to get hitched?"

"Now, Hetty, it's not such a crazy idea. You have a ranch to manage and a son who needs a father. I know Matt was doing his best to fill that role, but a boy needs a father."

"He has one."

Jacob looked around the room. "Where is he? Oh, that's right, he up and left you high and dry to raise your son on your own."

I gripped my coffee mug tighter, despite the heat against my skin, and I narrowed my eyes.

"Jacob, that was not a kind thing to say," Mama scolded him.

"But it's true."

John frowned at Jacob, and he pursed his lips. "I understand your hesitation. I've got several decades on you, and I know I ain't much to look at. We could be good friends. I would be a good father to Remington. Adopt him as my own."

He paused and reached for my hand. I pulled it away as his gaze softened.

"I would make him the heir to my ranch, as well as yours. I ain't getting any younger, and Jacob and I think it's time to think about the future. Matt was good to us. I see this as a small way to repay him for his kindness by taking care of you, Remington, and Tildy."

My gaze dropped to my coffee as I let his words settle. My gut reaction was a flat-out refusal. I read between the lines. He wanted Remi's ranch.

However, he would make Remi his heir. The size of both ranches combined captured my attention. My son would never want for anything. He'd be one of the largest ranchers in the area.

I looked at Mama, but I couldn't read her. Her eyes dropped to her pie, which she flaked apart with her fork. I turned my attention to John.

"I have some questions," I said, "that I'd like to discuss with you, John, in private. And I need some time before I decide."

John stood. "We can speak in your father's office, if you'd like."

I gave a curt nod. Then I stood and led the way. As I sat behind Papa's desk, John closed the door and took a seat across from me.

"Is this your idea or Jacob's?"

"Mine. And a bit of his. Like I said, we've been discussing what will happen with our place when he and I are gone, since neither of us has any children."

"Well, none that you claim."

He frowned.

"I am aware of your dalliances with the women of the Blue Diamond."

He lifted his chin and narrowed his eyes as he glared down the side of his nose.

"Do I understand not much would change should I agree with your proposal?"

"Like I said, I would not expect marital privileges."

"Let's be candid. I would not visit your bed. I would have my room separate from yours and you would *never* visit mine."

"Agreed."

"And I want a contract in writing about what we've discussed."

He nodded. Then he rubbed a hand on the top of his legs. "I would be a good father to Remington. And I would hope that you and I could be friends. We are both frank individuals who get to the heart of a matter."

"You're really going to name Remi your sole heir?"

He smiled. "Yes, I am."

"If, and it's still very much an 'if', I were to agree, I want to get to know you better before making a final decision. I know you as a kind neighbor who likes the painted ladies of the cat house. Those two attributes seem at odds with my way of thinking. So, before I involve my son in such a home life, I want the opportunity to assess your entire character."

"I think that is fair."

"And I don't want Jacob pressuring me. This is a matter between you, me, and my son."

John stood. "Agreed."

I let out a loud breath. "You've certainly given me a lot to ponder."

"How about I plan to come for supper on Sunday?" he suggested. "Give you and Tildy a chance to know me better."

My stomach tightened. "A week from Sunday would be better. Bring Jacob too."

He opened the door as I stood. I showed him to the dining room before I excused myself.

Then I hurried out to the barn. It was a strange request. I wondered what Mama thought about it. I could only imagine Papa's shock. Yet, John said he brought the idea to Papa long before Remi was born. Papa never said a word. That should tell me everything I needed to know.

I grabbed my saddle and gave Preston a brief nod before I rushed to White Lightning's stall.

"Let me do that for you," he said as he caught up to me.

As he took the saddle from my hands, I sighed. Seemed like all the men around me that day wanted to make decisions for me. I bit the inside of my cheek.

"You want some company?" he offered. "Won't take me but a minute to saddle up Ranger."

There was no harm in a horse ride, I guessed. "Fine."

While I waited for Preston to join me, I led White Lightning out of the barn and climbed into the saddle. When Preston sat atop his horse, I turned mine toward the southern pasture and let him run free.

As I leaned forward, close to his neck, I felt some of the anxiety lifting. By the time we finished our run and Preston caught up to us, I felt better, even though I still had no answers.

Preston laughed as he reined in his horse next to me.

"You didn't say you wanted to race."

"I suppose I didn't. You'll learn that White Lightning expects his morning run. He ain't happy until he has it."

"I'm sure he didn't like it when you were carrying Remi. No one to let him run free."

I snorted. "Who says I didn't?"

Preston raised an eyebrow.

I chortled. "Alright, you got me. For a few months, one of the cowboys took him out instead."

My shoulders slumped as I let out another long breath.

"What's on your mind?"

I glanced at Preston and almost let the whole bizarre story out. Instead, I lied. "Just missing my papa and his advice."

His eyes bored holes through my skull. As I shifted in my saddle, I looked away from his intense gaze.

"Just got some decisions to make."

"Now that sounds more like the truth of it."

When the silence lengthened between us, I looked toward the horizon. As far as my eyes could see, the land remained relatively flat, broken up by small ironwood trees and brush. The occasional wash scarred the grass-covered earth.

It was the only home I had ever known. If I married John, I was certain he would move us to his large house. Remi would forget what our home was like. He'd forget my papa. Once he took over the ranch, John's house would be his home.

And I'd be married to a man I didn't love. Shoot, I didn't know that I agreed with John's opinion that we'd be friends. It was all so very awkward.

What if the man who captured my heart so long ago got his life straightened out and I was tied to a man I didn't love? Where would I be then? Adultery didn't bother John, but it bothered me. Papa raised me better than that. Better than I had been.

Preston cleared his throat. "Been meaning to talk to you about Wednesday afternoons."

I turned my horse to make eye contact.

His eyes darted away. "Clyde has this meeting for men."

He took a deep breath and let it out slowly. "Men like me. Most have been sober for a while."

His eyes connected with mine. "Iris makes lunch. Then we talk for about an hour. It would take me away from the ranch for a few hours in the middle of the day—"

"I think you should go."

He cleared his throat. "Thank you for understanding."

"Well, I can't hardly tell you to stay dry and then stand in the way of you doing so."

"If you don't mind me asking, what did the Bartholomews want?"

I snorted. "A lot, as it turns out."

With that, I ended the conversation by kicking White Lightning into a gallop back toward the ranch. No way would I tell him about the proposal. If he found out on his own, that was fine by me. Just wouldn't hear it from my lips.

CHAPTER 9

PRESTON

The second Wednesday rolled around, and I fell into a routine at the ranch. Each morning, I fed and watered the horses, and I saddled Rio's horse. Then I helped Hetty train. I eventually gave up trying to convince her to stop.

In the afternoons, I cleaned out the stalls. Then I repaired things around the barn. I exercised the horses that remained behind, including Ranger. When the boys rode back in for the day, I cared for Rio's horse. Then I set the tack aside. After supper, I cleaned whatever tack needed it. Sometimes I ran into Hetty when she brought Remi out to look at the horses. Other nights, I didn't see her at all.

As I saddled Ranger, I couldn't keep my thoughts from her. She rarely smiled. It broke my heart because I remembered her as vibrant. Now she seemed like the entire weight of the ranch rested on her shoulders.

The sun warmed my back as I pointed Ranger toward town at a gentle lope. Thankfully, I left my duster behind. I would have been too hot.

For the first time, I yearned for a visit with people instead of the saloon. Even though the posse only met twice, they had become friends who cared about what happened to me. Last week I confessed how much I struggled the first few nights at the ranch and how relieved Hetty's new no-drinking-during-the-week rule made me feel.

As I reined Ranger to a stop in front of the Caldwell home, Clyde greeted me from the porch.

"Good to see you!"

I dismounted and tied Ranger to the post. He lapped water from the trough for a solid minute.

Then I shook Clyde's hand. "Glad to be here."

"How are the Clarks?"

"Good, I suppose. Hetty is determined to compete in the tournament in Prescott."

Clyde shook his head. "Wonder if I should pay her a visit."

"Might be good. She seems to have a lot on her mind."

"Well, come on in. Brian and Thomas are here already."

Both men greeted me with a handshake hug, the kind where they slapped me on the shoulder and released the hug quickly. My little sister called it a man hug.

Rich entered as Iris dished up the meal for us. As we sat down at the table, she ate on the porch.

Thomas offered the blessing. Then we dug in.

"Preston, how are you doing?" Rich asked.

"Alright. I've got a good routine established, like you suggested."

"Good. Day or night, if you're struggling, you head to my place. I know it's a bit of a ride, but I promise you, at some point, you will need to know someone's got your back. I expect you to take me up on it," Rich said.

"He's right," Brian said. "It'll sneak up on you. Everything will seem right as rain. Then 'bang'! Something triggers that old craving, and the next thing you know, it consumes your thoughts."

"When that happens," Thomas said, "You can't be alone. Find someone who knows what that's like—one of us."

"They're right," Clyde said. "You rely on us when that happens."

I frowned. "When, huh?"

All four of them nodded as Clyde reiterated, "When."

"If I've learned anything in a decade of sobriety, it can sneak up. Even with a long period without drinking. It's always gonna be a temptation. The sooner you come to terms with that, the easier it'll be."

"And the sooner you confront whatever set you on that path," Rich said, "the better. The less you let fester in your heart, the less there will be to drive you to the bottle."

I glanced down at my meal and took another bite. I didn't know what pushed me to drink.

They turned their attention toward Brian. He talked about his family and how demanding his father had been. How he felt like he could never live up to his father's unrealistic expectations.

A part of his story hit my heart. Not that my papa was like his. But I felt like I never measured up to my older brothers. James, Sam, Boone, and Deacon were all successful at their jobs. They didn't have darkness hanging over them like I did. It was always close by in the shadows, ready to swallow my soul with the least provocation.

"I was the youngest of five sons. I have one sister, eight years younger than me," I said. Then I told them all about my brothers. How I felt like I didn't matter. I was forgotten and invisible. "I could never be as good as them."

Clyde snorted. "I doubt they were as good as you make them sound. I'm sure they made a lot of mistakes and disappointed your parents as much as you think you did."

I frowned. "I am the rebellious one."

"Are you?" Rich challenged me. "Or is that just the mask you wear to protect your heart?"

My throat tightened and my breath shallowed as I wondered if there was any truth to what they said.

Thomas smiled. "You don't have to figure it all out today. When temptation lures you back to that dark place, think about it. Who is Preston Colter? Have you been playing a role, hiding your real self, to protect yourself? What would happen if you embraced who God made you to be?"

"It's very freeing," Brian said. "Once you accept yourself, that's when it gets easier."

I considered their words as I stood and started the water in the sink to wash dishes. Clyde helped me dry as the others headed back to work.

"Iris and I would love to have you join us for supper on Sunday after church, if you'd like."

"I suppose I could do that."

"And you're welcome to attend church as well."

I told him I'd consider it.

As I rode back to the ranch, I pondered their words.

———

On Sunday morning, I woke up early and hurried through most of my chores before breakfast. I saddled Ranger, White Lightning, and readied the buggy for Tildy and the Gallegoses.

When I returned to the bunkhouse, I grabbed a biscuit and stuffed some bacon and sausage into it. Then I took it with me as I led the horse and buggy to the main house. As I swallowed the last bite, I tied White Lightning to the post in front of the porch. Then I mounted Ranger and waited for the family.

"Morning," I said.

Hetty jumped a little. Then she smiled. "Thank you."

My heart raced at the sight of her. She wore a dark green dress that brought out the green of her eyes. I couldn't recall ever seeing Hetty in a dress.

"Should I return White Lightning?" I asked.

"No. This is perfect."

She mounted her white stallion despite the dress, revealing a bit of her ankles. I held back a smile. 'Course she'd ride astride in a dress.

"Horse!" Remi screamed and squirmed from Tildy's grip. "Horse!"

Hetty sighed. "Remi, you need to ride with Mimi."

Rio grabbed him by the waist and carted him back to the buggy.

"Horse!"

I cleared my throat. "He can ride with me."

Hetty flashed me a frown.

"My papa used to let me ride with him when I was little." It was something that I had forgotten and suddenly brought a bit of homesickness with it.

Her features softened. "Alright."

I held out my arms for the boy as Rio lifted him up. Then I settled him in front of me.

"Hold on to the horn like this." I showed him.

Remi giggled. "Horse!"

I laughed. "Yes, we're gonna ride the horse. His name is Ranger."

While I held the reins in one hand, I settled the other around Remi's waist to make sure he remained steady. My hand seemed gigantic compared to his little body. Then I nudged Ranger forward.

"Hold on tight. Don't let him fall." I heard the fear in Hetty's voice.

"Relax. I've got him."

When I glanced over my shoulder, I saw the doubt written all over her face. She kicked her horse forward. He snorted and nickered at the slow pace I set as she matched it.

"Go on. He'll be fine with me."

She sighed and let White Lightning run.

"Fast!" Remi giggled. "Mama fast!"

"Yes, your mama is burning the breeze," I agreed as I watched her long blond hair whip in the wind behind her.

There was nothing conventional about Hetty Clark. Never had been. That was part of her charm. Part of why I loved her.

The thought stabbed in my chest as I wondered just how much I really loved her. Would a man who loves a woman leave her? Disappear for years without a word? No. A selfish man acted that way.

As the truth made my gut squeeze under the guilt, I shift-ed in my saddle. I had done wrong by her. She was justified in her distrust of me. Her hurt was my fault.

I let out a slow breath as Remi snuggled back against me. After a minute, his breathing softened and his hold on the horn relaxed. I smiled. Her son was precious.

"You want me to take him?" Tildy said from the buggy next to me.

"Naw. I've got him."

For reasons I could not explain, I wanted to hold him close.

Before then, I never paid mind to children. Not my neph-ws. Sam had two boys before I disappeared from home. Probably had a few more by now. Boone and Jaclyn surely had a kid or two. I honestly didn't know. I lost touch with everyone.

The feelings stirring in me were hard to identify. I didn't feel this kind of connection with my nephews. But with Remi, I wanted to protect him. To spend time with him. To teach him things. It made no sense why this little boy took up space in my heart.

Perhaps it was because of his mother and my feelings for her. I wasn't sure.

When we pulled to a stop in front of the church, Hetty was waiting for us. She held out her arms for Remi.

"Come here, niño."

I handed him down to her and already felt a little sad.

"Rode horse," he said as he squirmed in her arms.

"It was fun, huh?"

He nodded emphatically, which brought a smile to my lips as I dismounted Ranger.

Once Rio reined in the buggy, I helped Tildy down.

"He's precious," she said. "And a joy. Looks a lot like his father."

My breath caught at her knowing look, and I wondered again if he might be my son. The thought terrified me. I was not a good man. Far from the man Remi needed to teach him about life.

CHAPTER 10

HETTY

As Preston stood frozen by the buggy, I asked, "You coming in?"

Whatever Mama said triggered something in him. The smile he wore while holding Remi disappeared, and fear filled his eyes.

He cleared his throat. "You go on. I'll be right along."

I smiled. "Thanks for letting Remi ride with you."

He nodded.

As confusion filled my heart, I turned and headed into the church. Watching Remi ride with Preston pulled at the strings of my heart. Since Preston showed up, I dared to hope that just maybe...

I shook my head. It was foolish to hope. He'd been sober for two weeks. It wouldn't last.

"Morning," Iris greeted me as I slid into our usual pew. "How are you holding up?"

I sighed. "Well enough, I suppose. I miss Papa more than I can say."

She smiled sympathetically before she greeted Mama. The two whispered for a few minutes before Iris greeted others.

I glanced over my shoulder. Preston sat in the back pew, looking like he was ready to fly the coop. Then the livery owner, Rich, greeted him and sat next to him. Preston's posture relaxed the longer they spoke. I was curious how they knew each other.

"Would it be too presumptuous to sit next to you?"

I startled at John Bartholomew's question.

"That's alright. I'll take the pew behind you."

"Morning, John," I greeted him at length. "I'm surprised to see you here."

Never once could I recall seeing him darken the doors of the church.

He snorted. "To be honest, I surprised myself."

I looked around for his brother.

"Jacob said he'd meet us at your place for supper."

When the music began, I focused my attention on the front of the church. Both the music and the message were a soothing balm for my fragmented soul that morning.

As soon as the service ended, I headed outside. Preston stood holding White Lightning's reins for me. I waited for Mama to settle in the buggy. Then I handed her Remi.

After I took the reins, I had almost mounted my horse when John's voice came from behind me.

"Need a hand up?"

"No, thank you."

He laughed. "You're something else, Hetty Clark."

"Ain't that the truth?" I muttered as I turned White Lightning toward home.

I nodded to Preston. "You coming?"

"Clyde and Iris invited me to stay for supper."

The disappointment I felt surprised me. "Have a good time."

"You too." He failed to hide the hurt in his voice as John rode up next to me.

"Shall we?" John asked.

"Let's go."

The ride home was pleasant enough. John talked about how he and his brother moved to Arizona from Texas about twenty years ago. They drove all their cattle through New Mexico to their current ranch. Built it from nothing, much like my papa had. That I had been Remi's age at the time John started his second ranch was not lost on me. He was older than Mama, which made him far too old for me.

By the time we arrived home, Jacob waited on the front porch. He helped Mama out of the buggy and followed her into the house. I dismounted, and Rio took the reins from me.

"Señorita, I'll take care of the horses," Rio said.

I thanked him and entered the house. John followed behind me.

"Rita needs a few minutes to finish supper," I said as I led him into the living room. "I'll warn you that Remi is usually pretty rowdy after church."

John laughed. "That's alright."

After I retrieved his blocks, Remi sat on the floor and played. He seemed a little shy around John. I should have expected that. He was a stranger to my son. I frowned at the thought. So was Preston, but he seemed drawn to him.

"What's wrong?" John asked.

I quickly masked my feelings. "Nothing."

"Horsey!" Remi squealed and ran to me.

I laughed. "Mama's wearing a dress today."

As I turned to John, I explained, "Sometimes I let him ride on my back as I crawl along the floor. I'm his horsey. Papa," my voice broke, "stood in on Sundays."

John smiled sympathetically. "I can give him a ride."

A lump lodged in my throat. I knew John was trying hard, but I wasn't sure I was ready. "That's alright. It won't hurt him to miss it this week."

John slid off his chair and onto all fours on the floor. "Come on, Remi."

Remi pressed against my legs and stuffed his thumb in his mouth. Awkwardness settled over the room. I would not force my son to do something he clearly didn't want to do.

"John, it's alright. He's shy around strangers. Once he knows you, he'll be ready."

He pulled himself back onto the chair with a few barely stifled groans. By the time he sat normally again, his face turned bright red. When his breathing slowed, he tried to laugh it off.

Thankfully, Rita saved us from further embarrassment. "Supper is ready."

Mama carried Remi as Jacob followed her. I stopped in front of John's chair and placed a hand on his shoulder.

"Thank you for trying. I appreciate it."

He gave me a half smile, then he stood and followed me into the dining room. He held my chair for me. Then he took the empty seat across from me. When Jacob reached for the platter of meat, Mama cleared her throat. His hand froze in mid-air.

"Hetty, would you say grace this afternoon?" she asked.

I bowed my head and mumbled some words of thanks. When I finished, I raised my head and smiled, despite the twisting in my gut. Even though John showed up at church, these men didn't share our faith. It was yet another issue.

Throughout the meal, I conversed politely with both Jacob and John, despite how anxious I felt inside. They were nice enough.

It was mid-afternoon by the time they left. I waited as they rode off in the distance. Then I hurried to my room and changed into a plaid shirt and denim trousers.

"I'm going for a ride," I said. "Can you watch Remi?"

Mama agreed, like always.

I slapped my hat down on my head. Then I practically ran to the stables. Preston still wasn't back, so I saddled my horse.

Once I was atop White Lightning, I pointed him north toward town without thinking. I pressed him for speed.

By the time I arrived, I was as winded as my steed. I needed advice, and I needed Clyde's perspective.

"Hetty? Is everything alright?" Preston asked as he hurried down the stairs.

The question hit an opening in the armor I kept around my heart. I slid off my horse as tears fell. I never cried, and as tears flowed down my face, I couldn't explain it.

Preston pulled me into his arms. My pulse raced as I absorbed the comfort he offered.

"What's wrong?" he whispered.

"Everything."

He laughed. "So, no one is hurt?"

I shook my head against his chest.

"Hetty?" Iris called as she joined us.

When I pulled away from Preston, I apologized. "I'm sorry. I don't know what came over me."

Impatiently, I swiped my sleeve across my face and eyes to dry my tears. I straightened my back and took a deep breath.

"I need to talk to Clyde and Iris," I said as my eyes locked with Preston's.

"You want me to wait for you?"

His question nearly caused my tears to overflow again. I

shook my head, even though I really wanted to ride back with him. He didn't move.

"Think I'll go visit with Rich for a bit," he said before he walked down the street. He left his horse tied in front of the parsonage.

"Come inside. Let's get some coffee and you tell us what's going on."

I barely sat down when I started explaining everything.

"John Bartholomew proposed."

Clyde frowned. "I was afraid that would happen."

My head jerked back in surprise.

He stared into his coffee for a second before his gaze met mine. "John has been after your father for years to bless a union with you. Matt wouldn't do it."

"He said nothing."

"Of course not," Iris interjected. "The entire notion is ridiculous."

I sipped my coffee.

"John is hunting for an heir. He knows most women won't put up with him. Before you were with child, he talked about a mail-order bride. Once your condition became known, he approached Matt. Suggested that he could adopt your child as his own. He was hoping you had a son."

My heart raced at the revelation that John's plan was years old.

"When Remington was born, he pressed Matt harder. Said anything and everything to convince him to let you marry John. So much that your father confided in us and asked our opinion."

I cleared my throat. "What did you tell him?"

"John only has his interests in mind. He wants Clark land. He wants to increase his holdings. Any discussion about making Remi his heir or providing for you is sweet talk."

Iris added, "John is too old for you, Hetty."

"I… I know that."

I looked down at my coffee as heat warmed my face.

"He promised you both ranches, didn't he?" Clyde asked.

"Yes. Remi would inherit them both."

Clyde shook his head. "I don't trust him."

I frowned as Clyde put words to the primary feeling I held toward John. Distrust.

"Don't let his sudden appearance at church bamboozle you. John isn't a church-going man. Never will be."

"Besides," Iris said. "I think there's someone else you would rather consider."

My head snapped up as I met her gaze. She knew Preston was Remi's father. I told her years ago. I couldn't believe she remembered that. Yet, the way she looked at me clarified she did.

"He's not someone I would ride the river with. He won't change."

Clyde cleared his throat. "I know better than you he can change. He's trying real hard."

I snorted. "Two weeks is hardly enough time."

"He wrote a letter to his family."

Iris's words hung in the air. I didn't want to believe that Preston might really change. If I did, then I would open my heart up for hurt when he failed.

"Said it's been years since he's written his mama. But after riding in with Remi this morning, he knew he needed to. It brought back some pleasant memories with his father."

"God is working on his heart," Clyde said. "And speedily. It surprised the both of us."

I lifted the coffee mug to my lips and took a long swig, unwilling to believe them.

"He loves you," Iris said.

I set the mug down with a clank.

"He wooed me, bedded me, and disappeared. He left me to raise his son alone."

"A fact which I regret very much," Preston said from the doorway.

My heart lodged in my throat. I pushed back from the table and tried to run past him, but he grabbed my arm.

"Running from things solves nothing," he said. "It's time we talked about this."

I jerked my arm from his grip. "You don't get to decide when I'm ready to talk to you, you skeezicks."

Then I rushed out of the house and mounted my horse. I let White Lightning have his freedom as we thundered out of town toward the ranch.

I didn't care if Preston regretted hurting me. It didn't change a thing. He left me. He left Remi. It was something I could not forgive.

CHAPTER 11

PRESTON

My heart crashed to the floor at Hetty's words. Remi was my son, and she was mad as a hornet with me for abandoning her.

When she broke my grip, my heart shattered. She hated me. I stood no chance of repairing the damage I had done. I had to follow her and make her understand.

Clyde's firm hand clamped down on my shoulder.

"Preston."

I froze.

"You need to let her go. You can't force her to forgive you. It's gonna take her some time."

"She still loves you," Iris said. "That's why she's so riled. Let it encourage you."

"And give her the time she needs."

My shoulders slumped. I wanted to mend our relationship. I wanted to do the right thing. To give her my name. To do my best to raise my son.

Son.

Air failed to fill my lungs fully. I had a son.

"Preston." Clyde's tone held a warning. "Don't travel

down that dark path."

When I found my voice, I stuttered. "I'm not. I'm... Remi is mine?"

I staggered into a chair.

"Yes. And sure, you made some mistakes but remember what we talked about. You can't let the regret and self-loathing take over."

"I... I know." And I wasn't. At least not right then.

Clyde and Iris each clasped one of my hands. Then they prayed over me. When they finished, I stood.

"I should head out."

"We'll be praying for you," Iris said as she followed me to the door.

As I rode home, the word itself floated over my heart like a warm blanket. Home. Clark Ranch was my home. Hetty was there. My son was there. It was where I belonged now. Whatever it took to make things right, I'd do it.

Lord, I don't know how.

———

As the days rolled into weeks and the end of June approached, the tension between Hetty and me faded. She accepted my advice as she trained for the competition. A time or two, she even smiled. She convinced me to train to compete as well.

Even though it was hard to work through the chasm of hurt between us, we bonded over broncos.

"Oof." She moaned as her backside landed hard on the ground.

I ran to get the horse under control. "How long was that?"

"Little over eight seconds," Pasqual, the cowboy that was

COLTER SONS BOOK 5

helping us practice, said.

Hetty smiled and let out a whoop.

I laughed. "Don't get too excited. You still got a ways to go."

"Don't steal my jubilation." She came over and fake punched my arm. "That was as fine as cream gravy, and you know it."

I gave her a half smile. "For a girl."

She narrowed her eyes. "Let's go again."

"No way. It's my turn. Let me show you how it's done."

I pushed past her and climbed onto the hurricane deck. She opened the chute. I read the horse's movements. My motion was as fluid as a gentle rain. Finally, around almost nine seconds, he bucked me off and I ate dust.

I hooted as I stood and brushed the dirt from my hat.

"Bet you can't beat that."

"We'll see about that, Colter."

Any time I riled her, she usually did her best. She was so competitive, and I loved it.

When her ride was done, she smiled. Sure enough, that ride was the best I'd seen her put up.

"I think you might just be ready."

She came over and nudged my shoulder. "You might be, too. And good thing, since we're leaving next week."

Pasqual took the bronco's reins from my hands, leaving me and Hetty alone in the corral. I wanted more than anything to pull her into my arms and plant a big kiss on those sassy lips.

Instead, I took a step back. It had been six weeks since she ran out of the Caldwell's house. Despite the progress we made, she wasn't ready for affection from me. I wasn't too sure she was ready to forgive me, either.

"That was a real decent ride. You looked smooth, but in

control."

When I turned toward the barn, she touched my arm. My breath left in a whoosh.

"Thank you."

As I pivoted to face her, my heart hoped hers softened toward me. I studied her green eyes. Those beautiful, shining eyes.

"For... Everything. Not pressing me about... Well, our past. And for helping me get ready for next week. I couldn't have done this without you."

She rested her hands at my waist. I placed one hand on her neck and I rubbed my thumb along her jawline. Then she gazed at me like she had in years past. As if I was someone important to her. When I lowered my head, she spun out of my hold, leaving an emptiness behind.

"Remi is on the porch."

I clasped her hand and led her into the barn. Then I spun her to face me.

"Was that a convenient excuse, or do you want me to kiss you?"

My pulse quickened as I waited for her answer.

"Want you to? Or think it's a good idea?"

"You tell me."

"I think it's a terrible idea." She pushed me away before she darted down the row of stalls toward the other door.

"As for your other question, I think you figured out the answer."

She grinned as she yanked the door open and disappeared from sight.

Yeah, she wanted me to kiss her. And she was right. It was a dunderheaded idea. Guess her mind won out over her heart that day.

"Preston!" Rio called for me from the doorway where

Hetty stood just a moment ago.

I ambled toward him.

"Got a letter for you."

I took the envelope and glanced at the return address. Mama.

My fingers shook as I opened the letter. Her first response came a few weeks ago. It had been short but encouraging. This one was much thicker. I sat on the stool by my workbench in the tack room as I slid the pages from the envelope.

Mama said how happy my last letter made Papa. He missed me.

I inhaled a shaky breath. I hadn't expected that. Perhaps he forgave me for what I did. For what drove me from the ranch.

As I let out a slow breath, I recalled what I wrote. I mentioned Remi, but only that he reminded me of the times Papa let me ride with him as a little boy. I didn't tell them he was my son.

"Your father says those are some of his favorite memories of you."

I blinked back the tears and wondered how I had ever thought that they forgot me or didn't love me anymore.

Mama told me about my brothers. James was courting Keri Glassman. Deacon was courting a young woman named Lilian Harper. I laughed out loud when I read Grady was courting Lilian's sister, Justine.

"Of course," I muttered. Grady wasn't my brother, but he was Deacon's best friend. It made complete sense to me they would end up falling in love with sisters. Anything else would have seemed wrong.

My younger sister, Vi, was growing up fast, according to Mama. She was fourteen and becoming a lovely young woman. I pitied any boy that showed an interest in her. With my brothers watching out for her, besides Papa, any young man must be on his best behavior.

"As you asked, I've said nothing to your brothers or sister about your visit. Although I wish you would let me tell them."

I glanced away from the words. I didn't want to set myself up for failure or get their hopes up in case I decided not to visit the ranch.

"We moved back into the old ranch house. We gave Sam and Ellie Mae the big house. With a fourth child on the way, they needed the space. You are welcome to stay with us, anyway. You can have Vi's room. She'll be happy to stay in the spare room at Sam's house. If that doesn't work, Deacon and Grady have an extra bed in their house."

I wasn't sure what I wanted. Seeing everyone would be nice. But staying with my brothers. I didn't think I could. Not after leaving like I had.

"Anyway, son, I love you and miss you. I'm so glad you wrote and that you're coming for a visit."

Mama signed her name with a flourish.

Slowly, I folded the letter and stuffed it back into the envelope. My shoulders rose and fell as I let out a long breath. Even though they seemed happy to see me again, I didn't know what to expect.

CHAPTER 12

HETTY

I stuffed a dress in my valise. Why a dress? I didn't know. I must have been cracked. When Preston said he wanted to visit his family's ranch while we were in Prescott, I decided Remi and I should go with him. Even if I didn't tell them Remi was their grandson, they would want to meet him.

Brushing a few loose strands of hair back from my face, I sighed. My heart was slipping away from me again. Training with Preston was wonderful. We smiled and teased each other. He almost kissed me once. And I wanted him to.

Thankfully, common sense won. He was just barely two months sober. I hoped he would make it through the coming trip to Prescott. The last two days, he seemed agitated, and it concerned me.

But his eyes were clear. I didn't think he was drinking. Yet, I was concerned the trip to Prescott might tempt him to start again.

"Hetty!" Mama hollered. "Stop dilly-dallying."

I snorted. It had been many years since Mama needed to scold me for being late. I closed my valise. Then I plopped my hat on my head.

"Coming!" I called out as I rushed down the hall.

"Here." I thrust the valise into Mama's hands. Then I went to pick up Remi, but he started running around the room.

"Please, Remi, come to Mama."

He continued to run as I sighed in frustration.

"We have to go," Preston said as he entered the house. He saw Remi and caught him by the waist. Then he mussed his hair. "Come on, squirt."

"Thank you." I said the words on an exhale.

Mama climbed into the wagon as I tossed my valise in the back. Judging by what we took, one would think we planned to be gone a month instead of a week.

When I mounted White Lightning, he pranced and fussed.

"Go on," Preston said. "I've got Remi."

All I did was point White Lightning toward town, and he took off like a bolt of lightning. After a few minutes, I made him run back to join our party, pulling up next to Preston.

"How you feeling?"

He glanced at me. "Nervous."

"Yes, that much is obvious."

He cleared his throat. "I didn't exactly leave on the best of terms."

"Oh? How long have you been gone?"

"Christmas time 1891."

A year and a half.

"You want to talk about it?"

He expelled a loud breath. "Yes, and no."

"Alright. I won't ring in."

"You want him for a minute?"

"Naw. He looks content in your arms."

I loved watching Remi ride with Preston. It made me long for what might be. No matter how I felt, Preston clearly loved his son. I wondered if that would be enough to keep him sober.

When we arrived in Ash Fork, the town bustled with activity, especially at the train station. Like us, several other area ranchers, cowboys, and their families headed south to Prescott. I dismounted near the stock cars. Then Preston handed me Remi.

Preston gathered the horses and checked them in, while Rio and Mateo unloaded the wagon. Then they delivered our bags to the attendant. Afterwards, Rio dropped our wagon and draft horse at the livery before joining us on the platform.

"You can feel the excitement," Mama said as she smiled. "I can't wait until we get there."

"Hetty!"

I swiveled toward the sound of my name. My throat tightened.

"John." I forced a smile. "Nice to see you. You headed down to Prescott?"

"Sure thing. So is Jacob."

As I waited for John to continue, I drummed my fingers against Remi's side.

"I'm sorry I haven't been by for a while."

I wasn't. I decided to give him the mitten and thought he figured that out. Apparently not.

"I was hoping we might talk alone."

Preston joined me and loosely looped an arm around my waist. His claiming me like that made me skittish. On one hand, it stopped John from saying more. On the other, I wasn't ready to be seen as a couple. There was no understanding between us.

"John," Preston said his name flatly.

John frowned and mumbled an excuse before he left.

"You never told him, did you?" Preston asked.

"I haven't seen him. Didn't want to make a special trip to his place just to turn him down."

He dropped his arm to his side and opened his mouth as if he'd say more but was cut off by the train whistle.

Folks started boarding the train. I stepped up, still holding tight to a squirmy Remi, as I found my seat. Then Preston sat next to me. He offered to take Remi, and I let him. Mama sat on the other side of the aisle next to a stranger. The sight tugged at my heart. It was the first year without Papa.

When everyone took their seats, the train pulled away from the station. For the first twenty minutes, neither Preston nor I said anything. At least Remi nodded off.

"I didn't leave on good terms." Preston's statement came out of nowhere.

As I shifted slightly to look at him, his gaze remained focused on the seat in front of him.

"I… I really hurt my family. My papa. My brother Sam. Even Deacon was angry, and he doesn't get angry about anything."

When he turned his face toward me, I saw the pain and regret. "You aren't the only one that I failed."

"It hurt me. I'm still a little hurt. But I can forgive you." I surprised myself by saying it out loud. "I'm certain they can too."

"But you don't know what I did."

I snorted. "I know what you did to me. And I can forgive that."

He faced forward and stared at his hands. When Remi

roused and pressed against Preston's arm, he looped it around my son's shoulders. Remi quickly fell asleep again.

That was the picture I longed for. My son with his father. His father by my side. If Preston proved he was a new man, maybe one day he might be my...

I cut off the half-formed thought. Just thinking about it would change how I felt about him, and I could not go there. Not until I knew he wouldn't destroy my heart.

Against my better judgement, I leaned against his arm. I hoped my closeness would give him the strength he needed to face the hard week ahead.

————

PRESTON

Inside, I felt balled up like a giant pile of twisted and knotted yarn. The only way to unwind it was to cut some extensive sections out. Yet that was exactly what I needed to do.

I wished I could talk to Rich or Clyde right then. This was the "when" that they warned me about, and none of them were around to help. I closed my eyes as Hetty leaned against my arm, drawing strength from her.

Lord, give me the strength to admit my failures to my family and to seek peace.

"Repay no one evil for evil," I whispered the verses that Rich made me memorize for this trip. "But give thought to do what is honorable in the sight of all. If possible, so far as it depends on you, live peaceably with all."

"Hmm. Those are good verses," Hetty whispered.

"Romans 12:17-18."

"And what honorable thing will you do with your family?" she asked.

"Ask forgiveness."

My gut twisted. I still hadn't asked hers. I hadn't done the honorable thing for her.

"Hetty…"

"It's alright, Preston. Don't deal with us right now. You have enough on your plate."

I lifted my arm and settled it around her shoulders. "But I should. I should have already asked for your forgiveness. Nothing I did back then was honorable."

She tilted her head up. "We both went too far. It resulted in this precious boy."

"I'm sorry I didn't stay. I'm sorry I left you—"

"I know. I… I forgave you some time ago."

My heart pounded against my ribcage as hard as if I had just rode the toughest bronco alive. She forgave me. Just like that.

"Now you gotta forgive yourself."

The truth of her words sliced deep. Wasn't that the hardest part? Forgiving the mongrel in the mirror.

CHAPTER 13

PRESTON

As the train pulled into Prescott in the late afternoon, the station platform filled with people jostling their way to the other side. Hetty held Remi in her arms as she stepped down from the train. I followed behind as the throng of people pressed around us.

"I'll get the horses," I said in her ear.

"Meet us at the Juniper House."

"Alright."

Then I pushed my way through the crowd to the stock cars. Several other wranglers and ranchers waited as horses were unloaded. A conductor directed us to a corral at the depot to pick up our animals. I followed the press toward the corral.

My skin crawled as I thought about being back in Prescott. The town charmed me with its Whiskey Row. My heart raced, and I wished again for the support of one of my posse friends.

"Franks!" one of the railroad men yelled above the din to announce their horses were available for pickup.

Several others were called before they called out Hetty's

ranch. I pushed my way to the corral and gathered the horses. Then I led them toward Uncle Thomas's livery. I had written ahead to reserve space for them, knowing how difficult it would be to find boarding once we arrived.

"Preston!" Thomas greeted me warmly. "Good to see you. You look well."

We chatted for a few minutes before I made my excuses. Then I paid him. The young man helping him led each of the horses to a stall.

My heart thundered in my ears as I walked past Whiskey Row. The music and revelry started early that day, most likely weary travelers looking to kill some time for the evening.

I crossed to the other side of the street and walked by the courthouse park, hoping the extra space would settle my cravings. Then I hurried to the Juniper House hotel.

When I arrived, Hetty stood outside with a grim expression on her face.

"They lost our reservation," she said.

I frowned. "Do you want me to talk to them?"

She narrowed her eyes. "Don't you think I can handle talking to a hotel manager?"

I held my hands up in surrender and stepped back. "Never mind."

"No one will have rooms," Tildy said. "What are we going to do?"

Oddly, our party looked to me as if I were suddenly in charge. My only idea was the last thing I wanted to do—go to Colter Ranch. I was afraid to show up at all, much less with my former lover, her mother, my son, and the Gallegoses in tow.

Hetty's shoulders slumped forward. I swallowed away the lump in my throat. It was the only option.

After I took off my hat, I ran a hand through my hair.

"Let's pick up the horses," I said as I stepped into the street.

Hetty grabbed my arm. "Why?"

"We're going to Colter Ranch," I said over my shoulder.

"Preston," she whispered my name.

I shook off her hold. "I'll be back with the horses. Wait here."

I jogged across the street, park, and back over to the livery. It surprised Thomas I was back so quickly. The saddles were still on the horses. When I told him I wouldn't need to board them after all, he offered to return the money.

"Hold on to it. I'll be back before we head home. If you haven't rented the stalls out, then you can keep it."

He thanked me before I left.

As I walked the horses down the street, I tried to ignore the draw of the rum holes and groggeries. My gut begged me to abandon everyone and hide in a glass of whiskey. If I did, then I wouldn't have to face my family yet.

Bringing home a bunch of strangers would surprise Mama, but she would accommodate everyone. I wondered if she would see Remi and know he was mine. I said nothing of the sort in my letters, however, rarely did a thing get past her eagle eye.

I doubted Papa would respond well. He'd ask to see me in the barn to riddle out my intentions toward Hetty and the boy. If he spoke to me at all.

Yes, going to the saloon instead of going home would be significantly easier at that moment.

But if I did that, I would lose Hetty and Remi and my job. If I chose them instead of the drink, she might reconcile with me and one day we could be an actual family. The longing wrapped my heart in a cocoon of hope. That hope propelled my feet past Whiskey Row and toward my son and my love.

When she spotted me, she blew out a loud breath. "You're back."

After some finagling, Rio and I secured the luggage on the back of the horses. It was less than ideal, but we were in a tight spot.

When we finished, Hetty said, "We don't have enough horses."

I gave her a brassy smile. "You want to ride with me?"

Her cheeks flushed pink. "You know, very few people can handle White Lightning."

"Alright. You want to take Remi or Tildy?"

"Señorita, Tildy can ride my horse," Rita volunteered. "I'll ride with Rio."

Rio grinned as he waggled his brows. "Si."

I gave Tildy a leg up. Once she settled, Hetty handed me Remi. Then she mounted her horse. I lifted Remi up to sit with his mama.

"You mind your mama, you hear?"

Remi nodded.

Then I mounted Ranger and led the way to Colter Ranch. The long ride seemed even longer than normal as my throat constricted.

Would they be happy to see me? Had they forgiven me? Or would my past indiscretions make the entire visit tense? I clenched my jaw as I tried to maintain control of the fear and doubt clawing at my mind.

My anxiety increased as we reached the hill overlooking Colter Ranch nestled in the valley below. Dusk darkened the sky. It was past suppertime, yet none of the people with me had eaten. I could not have planned a worse reunion with my family.

"Is this it?" Hetty asked with reverence tinging her tone.

"Yup."

A large man walked from the barn toward the Cahill house, followed by a lanky man. Deacon and Grady. I vaguely remembered Mama saying they lived in the old Cahill house and that Mama, Papa, and Vi were in the old ranch house. A lot had changed in the past one and a half years.

I clucked at Ranger and we headed down the lane we both knew by heart. Before we made it to the valley, Deacon and Grady turned around. Sam stepped out onto his porch, rifle at the ready. I couldn't blame him. They wouldn't expect to see me, much less with a group of people.

"Preston!" Papa's loud voice echoed across the valley as he ran toward me.

He ran. Toward me. Me. The rebellious troublemaker.

I barely pulled Ranger to a stop by the time he reached me. As I dismounted, he wrapped me in a tight bear hug.

"It *is* you."

Papa released me for a moment to study my face. Then back I went into a tight hug for several minutes.

"Hannah! It's Preston!"

Mama squealed. I could not recall Mama ever squealing before. Next thing I knew, she held me close. "My son is home."

My eyes burned. I coughed to keep my emotions suppressed. The homecoming was better than I hoped.

Mama released me and placed her hands on each side of my face. "You look good. Real good."

Her smile beamed across her face as tears trickled down her cheeks.

"I'm so glad you are home."

I cleared my throat. "Mama, I'm sorry for the inconvenience—"

"Don't say that. We are so glad to have you home."

I stepped aside so she could see the people I brought with me.

"There was a mixup with our hotel reservations. I…"

Mama wiped her cheeks on the corner of her apron. "Well, please introduce me to your friends."

I cleared my throat again as I lowered Remi from Hetty's arms before she dismounted. It felt good to hold on to someone. When she motioned to take him back, I pretended not to see.

"Mama, this is Hetty Clark, my employer."

"Hetty, welcome. We are so happy to meet you."

Mama pulled her into a hug, then released her quickly.

"And this is Tildy Clark," I said.

She gave Tildy an equally warm greeting. That was Mama. By the time we completed the introductions, she had adopted them as her own.

"Who do we have here?" Mama asked as she stood in front of me. She studied Remi's face. Then her eyes darted to mine. She raised one eyebrow.

I looked away as heat crept up my neck. She knew. "This is Remington Clark, Hetty's son. He goes by Remi."

"Well, you are a handsome boy, Remi."

When Hetty held out her arms, I released Remi. My anxiety heightened.

"Mama, I'm sorry to impose like this."

"Say nothing more. Come meet the rest of the family."

As Mama introduced Sam, Ellie Mae, their children, and so on, Papa stood beside me. He squeezed my shoulder like he was proud of me, something I rarely experienced.

"We didn't get the chance to eat," I whispered.

"Hannah!" Papa called. "Let's take these hungry travelers inside. Ellie Mae, do we have some leftovers?"

"We'll fix something up in a jiffy."

"Vi! Can you run home and bring over the pies from this morning?"

"Yes, Mama."

"Come on in," Sam said as he held the door.

I hung back, uncertain his welcome included me.

"You too."

As I walked past him, he hugged me. "Good to have you home."

I swallowed down the bitter regret. Out of all my brothers, Sam was the last person I expected to show me kindness. I tried to steal from him and Papa.

As Vi shuffled past me, I resisted the temptation to shake my head. She set the pies down on the table, then spun around and launched herself into my arms.

"I'm so glad you're home."

I hugged her and breathed in deeply, trying to accept the love of my family. I didn't deserve any of it.

"Come sit next to me," Vi said. "I want to hear everything you've been up to."

"Vi, we'll have time for that later. Help us with supper," Mama said.

Deacon and Grady excused themselves to take care of our horses before they headed back to their house.

Mama and Tildy hit it off nicely. Vi peppered Hetty with a dozen questions while she tried to eat. Ellie Mae engaged Rio and Rita. I sat there and picked at my food.

"Something wrong, son?" Papa asked.

I glanced at him. "Ah, no."

Then I stuffed some food in my mouth as I swallowed down the lie. Everything felt wrong. They should hate me.

They should have sent me packing instead of welcoming me and the strangers I brought with me.

When everyone finished eating, Rita stood. "Let me help clean up." She shooed Ellie Mae out of the way. "You see to your niños."

Ellie Mae thanked her and left to put her children to bed. It was getting late.

"Mama, do you think Maggie would mind if we offered their house to the Clarks?"

"Vi, that is an excellent idea. And no, they would not mind." Mama turned her attention to Tildy and Hetty. "There are three bedrooms with beds. Let's put you two and Remi over there."

"Remi can share with me for tonight," Hetty said.

"If there's a bunk open, I can take that," Rio offered. "Let Rita have one bed."

Rita smiled and squeezed Rio's hand.

"I can take a bunk, too," I offered.

"Oh no, Preston. You can take my bed," Vi offered.

My face warmed. I wasn't about to displace my little sister.

"There's an extra bed at Deacon's house. You can take that," Mama said.

I swallowed hard. I wasn't sure Deacon would care for that.

"Now, let's get out of Ellie Mae's house so her little ones will go to sleep."

Mama stood and motioned for everyone to follow her. Our things sat on the front porch, so Rio and I carried what we could. Papa helped.

"Where are the Larsons?" I asked, as we walked toward their house.

"George had a stroke a few weeks ago. During James's

birthday party. They are living with Melissa and her family in town."

"Is he alright?"

"Yes. Doubt they'll move back to the ranch. Maggie said if we needed use of their house, we're welcome to it."

I was sorry to hear about George's health. The Larsons had been longtime family friends.

Once the Clarks and Rita settled in, I headed over to Deacon's house. Papa walked in and explained he offered me the spare room.

I said little but took my things to the room. I still felt so unworthy of the kindness of my family. Despite the change of plans, it was nice to be away from the lure of the saloons. I wasn't sure I would have been able to resist them that night.

CHAPTER 14

HETTY

I still couldn't believe Preston took us to his family's ranch. Even harder to believe was how welcoming Hannah and Will Colter were, along with Preston's brother and sister-in-law.

As supper wound down, I glanced over at Preston. He looked sullen and remained quiet throughout most of the meal. I would have thought visiting his family would be a joyous occasion. It seemed like it was for everyone but him.

Once I put Remi to bed in the Larson's house, I sat out front on their porch. I heard someone leave the house next to me. As soon as I saw the red glow of a cigarette, I knew it was Preston.

As I walked over to that porch, I made a noise as I went so as not to startle him.

"You would be a terrible hunter," he muttered. "Heard you a mile away."

"Good thing I wasn't stalking any prey."

He leaned against the porch railing and took a long drag on his cigarette.

"Everyone settled in for the night?"

I smiled, even though it was too dark to be seen. "Yes. Thank you so much for bringing us here."

He grunted.

Once he finished his cigarette, I stood next to him. "What's on your mind?"

He groaned. "You aren't the only person I wronged, Hetty. Being back here is like barking at a knot."

"It seemed like your family was genuinely excited to see you."

He snorted. "They were putting on a good front for your benefit."

When I tried to slip my arm around his waist, he stiffened. I kept it there anyway. After a minute, he shifted away from me.

"You don't know what I did. If you did, you wouldn't be standing here."

I snorted. "I know what you did to me and I'm still standing here, aren't I?"

He turned to face me. "I stole horses from my brothers and my father."

The air left my lungs in a whoosh. I swallowed quickly to keep from coughing and tried to mask my surprise.

"It was late December '91. I was jingled out of my mind. I owed a dangerous man some money. A lot of money."

He coughed. "So, early one morning, I got up and saddled my horse. Then I took Papa, Sam, and Deacon's horses and headed up the lane toward town."

"It was just my luck that Ellie Mae woke early that day, too. She spotted me and woke up Sam. Sam and Papa came after me. They stopped me before I got to town."

His voice sounded desperate. "Don't you see? I stole from them. If it wasn't for Papa paying off my debt, I could have gone to jail or been hanging from a leafless tree with a rope around my neck."

"But you apologized, right?" I asked.

"No, I didn't. That morning was the last time I saw my family. Papa shoved my things in my saddlebags. He told me I should skedaddle and not come back. Both Sam and Deacon made sure I left the ranch."

My heart hurt for him. I didn't realize how much courage it took for him to bring us there.

"I'm even more thankful you thought of them when we needed a place to stay."

He cackled. "Why? You want to get in the middle of an old family feud?"

"No. I see it as a chance for you to clear the air. Set some things right with them."

Preston gripped the porch railing with his hands and pulled his body toward it. Then he pushed away.

"You should run far away from me. I'm no good. Haven't been for a long time."

As I closed my eyes, I prayed for words to say. Whether he was good or bad, I never cared. I just wanted him to remain sober and be himself.

I laid a hand on his arm. "What's that verse you told me on the train?"

"Do the honorable thing."

"And?"

"Do my best to live at peace with others."

"So, take this opportunity, this unplanned visit, to do just that. Ask your Papa's forgiveness. And Deacon's. And Sam's. And anyone else in the family that you've wronged."

"What if they reject me?"

I bit the inside of my cheek to stop the flow of tears that threatened at the rawness of his question. He found the core of his fear.

"The family I saw tonight will not reject you. They were sincerely joyous to see you without any confessions on your part. If that's not unconditional love, I don't know what is."

I rubbed a hand over his tense back.

"Asking forgiveness is just the gooey pie filling."

He snorted. "Gooey pie filling, huh?"

"Yeah, it's the best part."

"I'm more of a crust man, myself."

I hugged his arm against me. "Then it's the crust, or whatever metaphor makes you happy."

At last, he faced me and pulled me into his strong arms. Then he buried his head against my neck. I held onto him, content to comfort him. My, how I hoped he stayed sober. It was getting harder and harder to fathom life without him again.

"And that nonsense about not being a good man? That's what it is. Nonsense. Despite your past mistakes, in your heart, you are a good man."

He stiffened but didn't let go.

I whispered in his ear. "You are a good man."

He shook his head.

"You are a good man."

"Hetty…" his voice cracked.

"You are a good man."

He relaxed against me. Then the impossible happened. He broke down. My strong wrangler opened his heart to one small truth. He *was* a good man, worthy of his family's love.

———

The next morning, I donned my dress. I figured the

Colters were church-going people and since it was Sunday, I wanted to go with them.

Once I finished getting ready, I woke Remi and dressed him for the day. Then I carried him over to the big house.

The lake on the property sparkled in the early morning sun. I drank in its beauty while we walked.

"Morning!"

Hannah's voice drew my attention to the path between the small house and the big house. I hurried to catch up to her.

"Do you think your family would like to join us for service this morning?"

"Absolutely. Mama and Rita will be over for breakfast soon."

She studied Remi's face for a moment. "He's such a darling. Reminds me of Preston at that age."

Hannah placed a hand on Remi's back and sighed contentedly. Then she came back from wherever her thoughts carried her.

"Please come on in. I'm sure Ellie Mae has coffee ready."

When I entered, Ellie Mae greeted me with a hug.

"Vi is here already. She can watch Remington if you want to sit for some coffee while we make breakfast."

I handed Remi over to Vi. She played a game with her nephews and invited Remi. Once he warmed up to them, he joined in.

"So much like…" Hannah muttered.

"His father?" I asked.

Hannah's eyes locked on mine. I gave a nod. I was surprised she didn't press for details. Instead, she smiled, then she squeezed my hand as she set a steaming cup of coffee in front of me.

She turned back toward the kitchen and cracked several

eggs into a bowl.

"He always took a minute to warm up to new people. Sometimes I wonder if most of his life is lived inside of his head. He's so quiet. He holds too much in."

She cleared her throat and pasted on a smile as she whisked the eggs until they were smooth.

"How did he end up working at your ranch?"

"Ash Fork burned to the ground."

"I remember James mentioned that. In late April, right?" Ellie Mae said.

"Yes. A stranger pulled him out of a locked room in a burning building. The stranger didn't make it."

"Oh, my!" Hannah exclaimed as she poured the eggs into a warm skillet.

"He stayed with Pastor Caldwell for a week." I laughed. "I don't think he knew Clyde was the pastor at first."

"That's just like God, isn't it?" Hannah said.

"Anyway, Clyde, or maybe it was one of the other men in his group. Someone told him I was looking for a wrangler, especially since my papa passed."

"I'm so sorry for your loss."

"Thank you." I sipped my coffee for a few seconds. "He died saving someone from…"

Was Papa the stranger that saved Preston?

"The fire."

I gulped my coffee to hide my thoughts. Then I forced a smile.

"That was Papa. Always helping a person in need or taking in 'strays', as he called the strangers, that he gave a job. Some worked out. Some didn't."

I cleared my throat. "Anyway, Preston showed up on my doorstep looking for work. At first, I wasn't sure I wanted to hire him."

My voice faded as I looked to the parlor, where Remi played with his cousins. Boys he didn't even know were relations.

"I understand," Hannah said sympathetically.

"Anyway, I told him as long as he stayed sober, the job was his."

"And he's stayed sober?" Ellie Mae asked.

"Best I can tell, yes."

The smell of frying bacon made my stomach growl. I could eat a whole slab myself, as hungry as I was.

When the door opened, a line of men entered the house. Grady, Deacon, Preston, Sam, and Will brought up the rear.

"Horses are fed. We stopped by to invite Rio to breakfast. He'll be up in a bit," Will said.

A knock sounded at the door. Will opened it and welcomed Mama and Rita in.

Preston took a seat next to me.

"Thank you for talking to me last night," he whispered.

I squeezed his hand and smiled up at him as my heart grew closer and closer to his.

"You look beautiful this morning."

Heat warmed my cheeks and flutters danced in my stomach.

Rio entered the house right as the women set breakfast on the table.

The meal passed quickly. I offered to help with dishes, but the Colters wouldn't hear anything of it. So, I went out to the barn to saddle White Lightning.

"Thought you'd disappear on me?" Preston asked as he stood outside of the stall.

"Do I have time for a warmup ride?"

He grinned. "I think so. Let me saddle Ranger and I'll ride with you."

Within a few minutes, we were on the back of our horses. He kicked Ranger into a gallop, and I followed, easily overtaking him. I was pretty sure he let me catch up.

When I reined White Lightning in, he brought Ranger up next to me. I laughed breathlessly.

Then he nudged Ranger even closer and leaned over to me. He placed his hand on the back of my neck and drew me toward him. His eyes searched mine and all the air left my lungs. Then his lips brushed across mine firmly, sending my pulse racing. When he pulled away, I placed my hand on his neck and brought his lips back to mine. I kissed him like I hadn't seen him in years as I yearned for a fresh start with him.

White Lightning nickered and forced us apart. Heat warmed my entire face.

Preston grinned. Then, without a word, he kicked Ranger into motion and headed back to the big house.

I followed behind him, despite the warmth spreading through my middle and down my arms.

Attraction never had been our problem. On that morning, something deeper passed between us and I prayed, yet again, he would truly conquer the enticement of the bottle for good.

CHAPTER 15

PRESTON

The morning started out well. As I fed the horses before breakfast, I apologized to Papa, Sam, and Deacon. Each of them told me they forgave me some time ago.

"Mostly, we've been worried about you. No word for such a long time," Papa said. "Your mother and I pray for you every night."

I looked away, still ashamed of how I had hurt him.

Papa placed a hand on my shoulder. "I am happy to see you again. So are your mother and sister."

My brothers were out of earshot.

"So are they, even if they don't say it."

He squeezed my shoulder and gave it a good shake. "Our family isn't complete without you."

I frowned.

"Preston, those aren't just words. I mean it."

"Thank you, Papa."

Then he yanked me into the longest bear hug of my adult life.

When he released me, he said, "We ought to get on up to the house for breakfast before the women come hunting for us."

I followed behind my brothers as I tried to let his words penetrate the brokenness of my heart. Brokenness that I didn't understand.

During the time I met with my posse, I figured out pretty quickly that a lot of my brokenness had no clear root. Unlike my friends, I grew up in a wonderful home with loving parents. Sure, my big brothers picked on me. Boone more than the others. But none of it made sense why I drank my feelings away.

Perhaps I was as crazy as popcorn on a hot stove. Yet, when I was sober, I often felt lower than most people around me. I was rarely happy. Rarely excited. Rarely up. My default state was a little down.

When I entered the big house, I smiled at the sight of Hetty in a dress. Only on Sundays. Frankly, I didn't care what she wore. She looked good in any outfit.

I took a seat next to her. "You look beautiful this morning."

Her face blushed, which made her green eyes sparkle.

Her words to me last night still rang in my ears. *You're a good man.* I didn't feel it. I barely believed she said it. Especially since I was the reason she lost so much. Even though I disappeared and left her to raise our son alone, she still believed in me. Saw something good in me.

Once breakfast finished, I went outside for a smoke. I watched as Hetty walked to the barn alone. I hurried to catch up.

While she saddled White Lightning, I made some witty comment and saddled Ranger. Then we rode out together.

When she stopped, her face glowed. It had been years since she looked that happy. She laughed, which made me want to kiss her. So, I positioned Ranger next to her as I leaned close.

She didn't shy away from my touch. Her expression betrayed her heart. She loved me. Still. After everything.

Then I kissed her. Not like I wanted to. Just a quick brush of my lips on hers. Only she captured me before I pulled away. Her kiss lit the embers of my heart, renewing my love for her. Not the infatuation of our youth. I truly loved her. I wanted to spend the rest of my life with her.

When she ended the kiss, I grinned as joy seeped into my bones for the first time in years. There was hope for us.

Then I rode back to the big house. The men in my family headed to the barn to saddle horses and hitch up the wagon.

I dismounted in front of the house. Then I entered and found Remi. "You want to ride with me to church?"

"Horse man!" he giggled.

"Sounds like that's a yes."

Mama's laughter hung in the air. "Horse man?"

I lifted Remi into my arms and carried him over to my mama. "Hetty was explaining to him I was the wrangler. The man who takes care of the horses. Somehow, he turned that into 'horse man'."

Mama smiled. "He's a darling."

"Do you want to hold him?"

Mama's blue eyes locked on mine. Same blue as mine. Same as Remi's. She had to know.

She nodded.

Once Remi was in her arms, he hugged her tightly. Mama's eyes misted. She definitely knew. Only she was too kind to say anything. She held him for another minute before she gave him back to me.

"He reminds me of you at that age," she whispered as she straightened my hat.

Then she took a deep breath. "Your father is probably waiting. We should go."

I held the door open, and she stepped onto the porch.

Everyone from Clark Ranch went with my family to church. I met Grady's fiancée, Justine Harper, and Deacon's sweetheart, Lilian Harper, and their siblings. Boone, Jaclyn, and their baby, Jaxson, were also there. As the service started, I was thankful I didn't have to dwell on the anxiety I felt around Boone.

After service, we all returned to Colter Ranch, including Boone's family and all the Harpers. Rio and I helped my brothers set up some makeshift picnic tables outside. I forgot how noisy Sunday supper was, especially with several little ones around.

Vi gathered all the children around her and Jaclyn, letting Ellie Mae have a break from her three children. Deacon didn't want to let go of our niece, Ashley. It was strange watching my tall, beefy brother holding the sweet infant. Just as strange to see Boone holding his son.

The conversation hummed, but I only took part when directly asked a question. Suddenly, I felt like an outsider.

"You competing?" Boone asked.

I looked up at his question. "Both Hetty and I are competing. Broncos."

Boone grinned. "Hetty, you won a few years in a row, if I remember."

"Yes. Both '89 and '90. This is my first year back since Remi was born."

Boone's smile faded as he glanced over at the children's table. His eyebrows rose. Then he quickly recovered with a forced smile instead.

"Looks like he gets along with the others pretty well."

I snorted and muttered under my breath. "Unlike us."

Boone frowned. "Come on, Preston. We were just boys. You were too young to remember that James picked on me for many years. He only stopped when I grew big enough to stand up to him."

"Explains a lot," I said flatly.

In my case, I never got big enough for Boone to stop. It wasn't until he married Jaclyn and moved out that the endless teasing and pranking stopped.

Hetty laid a hand on my arm and I shut my trap.

"What do you do for a living?" Hetty asked Boone, which effectively ended our argument.

After I left the table, I walked over to the lake. I pulled a cigarette from my case and lit it. Then I studied the rock formations surrounding the lake as if I saw them for the first time.

Perhaps the animosity I felt toward Boone was part of why I hid away in the bottle. There wasn't a day during my childhood and my teenage years where he didn't pick on me. Sometimes he cajoled Deacon into his antics. Other times, it was just him. He picked fights. Wrestled me to the ground and wouldn't let me up when I begged him to stop.

"Maybe I should have stepped in more, especially since Boone and Deacon were so much bigger than you," Papa said as he propped his foot on a rock nearby.

I frowned. "Maybe you should have."

"I just figured you boys were roughhousing like boys do. I never saw how much it hurt your heart."

I took a drag of my cigarette and flicked the dead ashes on the ground.

"I'm sorry, Preston."

I took another drag as a battle waged in me. The little boy tortured by his brothers cried. He was angry that no one stood up for him. The man in me saw my papa's humility. I doubted Papa deserved any of the blame.

"They were old enough to know better."

"Still, I could have done more."

Then Papa cleared his throat. "I'm glad you're here. How long can you stay?"

"Tomorrow, Hetty and I will register for the competition and stay to practice. Then Tuesday is the competition. Our train tickets are for the morning train on Thursday."

"It's good to watch you with your son."

I crushed my cigarette in the dirt and straightened my back. "Who told you?"

"Hannah and I figured it out on our own. It was when you went on that surveying trip with Boone."

It wasn't a question.

"How long have you known you had a son?"

I cleared my throat. "I only found out after I started working for Hetty. She couldn't find me to let me know."

"They grow up fast, you know." His voice held a hint of regret.

I blinked and forced my gaze to remain on the scenery.

"Seems like you and Hetty are getting along alright, especially if that kiss this morning is any sign."

My face warmed. "You saw that?"

"So did your mother."

As he danced around the topic, I figured he wanted to know if I planned to marry her. For Papa, only one choice was the right one.

"It's not up to me," I said, as if he had asked the question. I angled to face him.

"I've only been sober two months. She doesn't believe that I'll stay off the sauce. I can't blame her. I'm not so sure that I can change forever."

I snorted. "It's ironic. When I was locked inside the

burning building, I bargained with God. I promised to change if he'd get me out of there. I didn't know it'd be like trying to scratch my ear with my elbow."

Papa placed a hand on my shoulder, like he often did during a father-to-son talk. Then he released it.

"I'm living proof that it is possible."

I snorted. "You never drank a drop in your life."

Papa shook his head. "That's not true. You are more like me than you realize."

My heart thudded in my chest as I listened to him explain.

"Long before I met Hannah, way back when I was your age, I spent most weekends at the bit house with the ladies of the line."

He cleared his throat. "Remember how you showed up at Christmas time in '90? Almost died from being deep in your cups? I can't tell you how many brushes with death I had. My father pulled me out of the saloon many times."

I wasn't sure I believed him. My papa was the most upright man I knew.

"I can see you're trying to make sense of it. Let me say this: I experienced a pivotal moment, much like you did, that woke me up. I saw the direction my life was heading, and I resolved to be different. The first few years were very hard. An argument with my brother, or nearly any little thing, threatened my resolve."

His eyes softened.

"I didn't have friends like you have. Just my papa and your Aunt Julia helped some. I didn't let them in for many years. I cowboyed up and gritted through it. By the time I left Texas and started this ranch, I had many years of success under my belt."

"So, you just never drank again?" I wanted to believe it

could be true.

"It wasn't easy. The temptation never truly goes away. But the more time and distance between me and the bottle made it easier to choose wisely. There were times it was hard. When Sam was kidnapped. When your mother was very ill. When she almost miscarried you. When you almost died at Christmas time. Sometimes problems arose with the herd and it was one thing after another after another."

"The temptation was still there. The whisper of a promise to detach from reality. But I knew if I went there, I would lose my wife and my children. It wasn't worth the cost. So I prayed instead. I didn't know what to say. Sometimes it was a simple cry for help. Other times, I learned to pour out my heart to God."

He squeezed my shoulder. "Do you hear what I'm trying to tell you, Preston?"

"Is it possible to stop for good?"

"Yes. And if you weigh the cost of giving in, you will learn what is most important to you."

That was easy. Remi. Hetty. I wanted to marry Hetty and be a family. I wanted us to have more children and to run her ranch together.

Squeals from the boys caught my attention as Boone strip-ped down to his underthings and ran into the lake. It surprise-ed me he hadn't dived in buck naked.

Papa laughed. "See, even Boone can change."

Sam took his sons in for a dip. Deacon, Grady, and the Harper boys joined them.

"You should go teach your son how to swim. Enjoy the time you have with him. He'll grow up before you know it."

"You coming?"

"Naw. I'll watch from here."

After that, I found Remi, and we enjoyed an afternoon swimming in the lake. His giggles echoed in the breeze and warmed my soul.

CHAPTER 16

HETTY

Monday morning Preston and I left immediately follow-ing breakfast. As we rode into town, I relished the peaceful feeling.

"It was fun watching you swim with Remi."

Preston chuckled. "I think he finally caught on by the time we were done. Too bad there aren't any lakes nearby home."

When I realized my ranch was the home he referred to, I smiled.

As we neared, we heard the noise from town several minutes before we saw the crowds. Once we arrived, we wound through the streets to the rodeo grounds. Then we stabled our horses in their barn before taking our place in line.

When we discovered there was a separate line for the women's competition, I stood in the short line. Once I reg-istered, I stood in line with Preston while he waited.

Long before we made it to the front of the line, I saw John Bartholomew headed our way.

"Hetty! I've been looking all over town for you for

days."

I held back a snort. I was pretty sure that wasn't true.

"We need to talk," he said as he pulled on my arm.

"I'll be back in a minute," I said to Preston.

"What do you want, John?"

"An answer to my proposal."

"No."

When I spun on my heel, he grabbed my arm.

"Hetty, come now. Let's be reasonable. You don't think that your wrangler has a hope in Hades of staying out of his cups, do you?"

I shook off his grip and frowned.

"Remi needs a better role model than him."

"A man who spends his nights at a brothel is better?" I scoffed.

John's eyebrows drew together, and he stepped closer to me. His breath was hot against my face. "I've tried to reason with you, but you're being stubborn. Make no mistake. I will make you my wife."

I balled my hand into a fist and drew back my arm before I hit his stomach with my hardest blow. Then I stomped down on the arch of his foot.

"Over my dead body," I growled and walked away leaving him to hobble in the opposite direction.

When I joined Preston again, he said, "I take it you refused his proposal."

"He doesn't understand the meaning of the word 'no.' I'm tempted to hold on to that useless parcel of land just to spite him now."

"Remind me not to make you angry."

As he rubbed a hand on my back, I calmed down. A few minutes later, we reached the front of the line. Preston's practice time was only a half hour from then. Mine was scheduled for late afternoon.

So, we found a spot in the bleachers to watch while he waited for his turn. The handlers brought in an unruly brown mare. It bucked the first rider of the day off in less than qualifying time. When he tried a second time, the mare grassed him in three seconds. He laid on the ground for several minutes before two men carried him out.

My stomach tightened. "Be careful, Preston. She looks dangerous."

He flashed a cocky grin. "Don't worry. I know what I'm doing. I'll be fine."

"Colter! You're on deck."

I wrung my hands as Preston left my side. The second rider fared no better than the first. At least he limped away after his second attempt.

As Preston climbed onto the mare's back, he rubbed her neck and whispered to her. Then he closed his eyes for a second.

After the gate burst open, I held my breath. She lunged and kicked and bucked violently. Four seconds. Another jolt. Preston was still on her back. Five. Six. Then she went wild. He flew over her head, landing face first in the dirt.

I stuffed my fist in my mouth to keep from screaming out. When he slowly stood up, I breathed again. Then he brushed the dirt from his shirt and pants. His furious eyes could have burned down an entire forest.

Before the handlers loaded her into the chute, he asked to inspect the mare. I couldn't hear what he said, but his frown remained in place during a heated exchange with the handlers. Then he waved the judge over. The judge inspected the horse and said a few stern words to the handlers before they took the horse away.

Preston rubbed his low back while he waited for a replacement. The gray mare they brought out looked just as fierce. After the judge and Preston inspected the horse, they loaded her into the chute. Preston eased into the saddle. He took a deep breath, then let it out slowly. At his sharp nod, the gate opened.

The gray mare lunged out of the chute. Her style was like our bronc. Preston easily read her moves. Six seconds. Seven. I held my breath. Eight. Nine. One powerful jolt and she rid herself of my man.

Preston landed on his rear. As he jumped to his feet, he grinned. Nine and a half seconds. The other men watching nearby murmured. When he waved to me, I doffed my hat and smiled.

A few minutes later, he sat with me, and we watched the rest of the men as they practiced. None of them beat Preston's time.

"You might just pull out a win tomorrow," I said as I nudged his arm.

He laughed. "You know as well as I do, any ride can turn out much differently than expected."

"How are the first two men?"

Preston shook his head. "The first man won't be competing. Broke his arm and got a concussion."

"Oh, no!"

"Second one is still hurting pretty bad. Said he'll decide tomorrow."

"What about the horse?"

"She won't be in the rotation."

I didn't press for further details. As familiar as he was with horses, I was glad he recognized a problem with the animal and that the judge listened.

Around noon, we walked to the food booths near the rodeo grounds. I ordered a sandwich and grabbed some water. Preston did too, before we found a spot in the shade of a tree. He groaned as he crouched down.

"Gonna be sore for a few days from that one."

"You sure you're alright?"

He nodded. Then he bit into his sandwich.

"Nine and a half seconds is the time to beat." I winked at him. "I'll see what I can do."

He swallowed a bite of his sandwich. "What did John say to you before you punched him in the gut?"

"He told me I will marry him."

Preston frowned. "Just how does he figure he can force you to marry him?"

"Don't plan to find out."

"Hetty, be careful. I don't trust him. Or his brother."

"Don't think Papa did either."

I told him about my conversation with Clyde. "Apparently, John has been after me for years and I didn't know it."

Preston studied me for a minute while I ate. At length, he finally said, "You know, if you were already married, he could do nothing about it."

My heart pounded against my chest as if it agreed completely. My head wasn't so eager.

"I don't know."

He reached over and took my hand in his. "Would it be so bad to marry me?"

I glanced away. "Not if you stay sober."

As he released my hands, his shoulders slumped. Any hint of love or happiness erased from his face.

"And there it is. How long before you'd be willing to consider it?"

I scrunched my face. "I don't know. Two months and two weeks doesn't sound long enough."

He stood abruptly. "So you trust me with our son, even

though you don't believe in me?"

I stood and brushed the dirt from my trousers. "I didn't say I don't believe in you."

"You don't have to. It's written all over your face. It's screaming in the tone of your voice. You do not trust me to change."

I turned away. "I need to go. My practice ride is soon."

He called after me. "Just so we're clear, you're the one running away, not me. Not me!"

As I hurried away, I bit the inside of my cheek. I practically sprinted back to the ring where they brought out a dark brown mare. She looked more docile than the one they used for the men, which only added to my frustration as I prepared for my ride. I wanted to ride the same horse as Preston.

I waited my turn as the first three women practiced. Yup. That mare was definitely gentler than the gray mare.

I stormed over to the judge. "I want the gray mare from this morning."

"You can't ride her."

"Why not?"

"She's earmarked for the men's competition. You get this one."

"She's weak."

The judge narrowed his eyes. "Lucky you. You'll put up some good numbers then."

As I started to protest, he stopped me. "You ride the horse we provide or you forfeit."

I pursed my lips and stomped back to the waiting area.

"Clark! You're up."

Once I mounted the horse, I could tell she was significantly milder than my bronco. I held back my frustration. Then I took a deep breath and leaned forward. I raised my left arm and nodded.

When the gate opened, she pitched forward. Then she tossed her back end in the air. She felt slow and too easy to predict. I was certainly long past the eight seconds. In fact, the judge called time before she forced me off.

I dismounted and headed toward the judge.

"You call that a bronco?"

He stepped closer to me. "You got one practice run left. You want to use it?"

"Yes, but with the gray mare."

"I already told—"

"What's the harm?" Preston said.

I glared at him. It was my battle, and I didn't want his help.

The judge startled. "You want to chance her beating your time?"

"Don't matter to me. If she's a better rider, then so be it."

"Fine." The judge shook his head. He walked over to the handlers and asked them for the gray mare.

I lifted my chin and straightened my back. I could do it.

"Remember," Preston said. "Slightly forward. Watch her bounce to the left."

I grunted. Then I took my place on the back of the sturdy mare. I instantly noticed the difference. She was a true bronco. Wild at heart. Just like me.

Slowly, I let out a breath. Then I raised my left arm and dug my spurs into her side right as the gate flew open.

"You got it, Hetty!"

Forward. Lean back. Forward.

She bucked left, so I leaned slightly right to counterbalance.

"Eight!"

Her rear bounced violently. She put up a good fight.

"Nine!" Preston shouted to me.

Forward. Back. Up. Down.

"Nine and a quarter."

Almost there.

A hard shock and I flew off her back.

Preston hauled me to my feet with a huge grin on his face. "You did it!"

As I tried to catch my breath, I rubbed my backside.

"You beat me by a tenth of a second," he said as he pulled me into his arms and twirled me around. "I knew you could do it."

Then, in front of all the competitors, he crushed his lips against mine. *Guess he didn't mind being beaten by a girl*, I thought as I surrendered to his kiss.

CHAPTER 17

PRESTON

I couldn't be prouder of Hetty. It didn't bother me in the least that she beat every bronco rider in the tournament. She proved what I knew: she was as tough as nails.

Without thinking, I pulled her into my arms and kissed her. Some men hooted and hollered. When I finally released her, we were both breathless.

"I beat you fair and square, Colter."

I grinned. "Yes, ma'am, you did. Now, tomorrow, you'll have to do better."

"You bet I will."

We walked back to the waiting area. The last woman to practice rode the easy mare and put up decent numbers, but nothing like Hetty's. All things being equal, Hetty would win tomorrow.

It was late afternoon by the time we saddled up for Colter Ranch. My lower back hurt something fierce, and I kept shifting in my saddle. When I dismounted, I moaned.

"You gonna be alright for tomorrow?" she asked.

"I'll see if Mama has something to help."

When Mama saw me limping toward the house, she

scolded me. "You're hurt."

Then she grabbed her medical bag. "I'll make some willow bark tea for now. After supper, I can mix up a salve that might help."

"Thanks, Mama."

The next morning, I was still stiff and sore. With the way I felt, I doubted my times would look as good as yesterday. Hetty and I lagged at the ranch even though we'd miss the morning baseball game. I needed the extra time to work out the kinks in my back and legs.

We finally arrived in town around eleven. The women's competition was up first, so my family joined me in the stands to watch Hetty compete.

They used the same dark brown mare from yesterday. I thought it wasn't fair to use such a tame bronco. We watched as the other four women competed. The mare was as sluggish as the day before.

Then Hetty's turn came.

"Mama!" Remi screamed from Tildy's arms.

I smiled as Hetty's gaze found me. I winked. She had this.

After she went through her warmup routine, she leaned forward and nodded.

The gate opened, and the mare lurched forward. Hetty dug her spurs in deep, finding the right pressure to make a show of it. She looked fluid on the back of the mare, easily anticipating the horse's movement.

Eight. Nine. Ten.

My heart pounded.

When the mare reared up, Hetty dropped off her back and she landed on her feet. Never seen that before.

The crowd cheered. She won, hands down. Didn't need to hear the results to know it. Hetty took a bow. Then shook the hands of the other competitors.

I was so proud of her, even though I knew she preferred a tougher mare. In the end, she won first place and the tidy sum that went with it.

I scooped Remi up in my arms. "Let's go find your mama."

"Horse man!"

I chuckled.

When we caught up to Hetty, her cheeks flushed pink with excitement. The glimmer in her eyes brought a smile to my face.

"Mama!"

"Hey, Remi," she said as she took him. "Mama won."

He smiled as big as hers.

Then I pulled them both close and placed a kiss on Hetty's cheek. "You did it. I knew you would."

She winked at me. "Now let's see how you do."

The men's competition started, so I let her go. She joined my family in the stands. My assigned spot was toward the tail end. The longer I stood there, the more my back hurt, so I paced back and forth to loosen it up.

When I climbed on the back of the gray mare, my tailbone complained. I took a deep breath and leaned forward as a twinge of lightning traveled down my leg. My breath exhaled quickly.

Without waiting for my signal, the handlers threw open the gate. The mare raced out and bucked hard. I almost fell off before the qualifying time. Instead, I angled left to correct my posture. She jerked forward. Then pushed up her hind end. I held on for dear life. It was not the ride I hoped to put up.

Suddenly, she bucked sideways, and I flew off her back and landed close to her with my face in the dirt. When her hoof came down, it landed on my calf. I howled at the pain and curled up in a ball, grasping my leg. The pain sucked me under as I heard Hetty scream out my name.

———

HETTY

I shoved my son toward my mother. Then I jumped over the railing separating the stands from the arena. I ran toward Preston's still form. Since the anger stopped my tears, I let it come.

When the handlers finally controlled the horse, I dropped to my knees next to him. His arms fell to his sides as I rolled him over. The tear in his pants exposed a deep purple bruise.

"Ma'am," a man said next to me. "Let me look."

When I noticed the black bag in his hands, I scooted out of the way. Everyone in the arena silenced.

The doctor felt Preston's leg. Then he checked him for other signs of injury. I held my breath as the exam seemed to take forever. The doctor motioned some men over. They rolled Preston onto a stretcher. I followed him as they carried his still form back where the contestants waited.

His father and mother tried to push their way past some guards.

"Let them in," I said. "They're his parents."

The men let them pass.

Hannah knelt next to Preston and held his hand. Will crouched beside them and placed an arm around his wife.

"I think the pain caused him to pass out," the doctor said. "When he comes to, give him some of this."

The doctor held out a bottle of whiskey.

"Absolutely not. Do you have some willow bark powder?" she asked.

The doctor frowned. "It's not as strong."

"It'll be better for him in the long run," Will said.

The doctor handed Hannah a small vial of the powder. He said the leg might swell but should heal in a few days to a week.

When Preston groaned, I let out a loud breath.

Will left and quickly returned with some water. Hannah mixed in some willow bark powder.

"Here, sip this," she said as he sat up.

He did as she instructed.

"How did I do?"

I growled. "How about 'are you alright'?"

He gave me a saucy grin. "You know you'd ask the same thing."

I harrumphed. "You placed third."

He shook his head. "It wasn't my best performance."

"No, but still good enough to place. You scared me."

He snorted. "It ain't no fun to get stepped on by a horse."

"Well, don't do that again."

"Don't want to ruin anyone's day, but I'd like to head back to the ranch."

The worry on Hannah's face eased.

"Don't think you should ride a horse, son," Will said.

"I can take him back," I volunteered.

"Señorita, I will drive the wagon," Rio said. "Then I can bring it back to town."

Hannah clearly wanted to come too but said nothing. Instead, she handed me the vial of powder.

"Don't go up any stairs," she warned him. "Just take it easy."

"I'll make sure of it," I said.

Will and Rio helped him back to the Colter's wagon. When I found Mama, she agreed to keep Remi with her. Then I retrieved White Lightning and Ranger and rode next to the wagon.

Once we arrived back at the ranch, Rio pulled the wagon up to the Larson's home, as it had some nice beds and no stairs. He and I helped Preston to the closest room. Then Rio offered to take care of our horses and I let him.

I mixed up more of the willow bark powder and gave it to Preston. After he finished it, he leaned back on the bed.

"You should go to sleep," I suggested.

He tugged on my arm. "Sit with me."

I eyed him warily. "Trying to get me into your bed again?"

He chuckled. "I'm pretty sure you have nothing to fear."

When I snuggled up next to him, he placed an arm around me. Within minutes, his arm relaxed and his breathing grew soft. I carefully sat up and brushed his hair back from his forehead.

Then I let the emotions come. Tears streamed down my face. I could have lost him. That horse's hoof could have come down on his skull. He could have died. Then Remi would truly not have a father. I leaned over and kissed his cheek.

After I left, I walked around the lake to calm my spirit. His childhood home was so beautiful and peaceful. His parents were incredibly gracious. I smiled as I thought of each of his siblings. In their own way, they all welcomed me with open arms.

No secrets remained. His parents figured out Remi was Preston's son. I felt no need to pretend otherwise. I ought to let Remi get to know them. Since Preston was in rough shape, Remi and I could stay behind and spend more time with his family. There was no need to rush back to my ranch.

CHAPTER 18

PRESTON

I slept the rest of Independence Day and didn't wake until the morning after. My leg and back both hurt. As I opened my eyes, I groaned.

"Hello handsome."

Hetty. I wouldn't mind waking up to her beautiful face every day.

"Care for some willow bark powder?"

She helped me sit up and then she handed me the mug without waiting for my response. I sipped the liquid and hoped it would dull the pain in my calf soon.

As she sat on the edge of the bed, her gaze roamed over my face.

"What?"

"I think we should stop riding broncos."

I laughed. "Hetty Clark, I couldn't agree more. Let's not leave Remi without parents."

"My thoughts exactly."

"Speaking of my son…" It was the first time I said the words out loud, and I liked the feel of them.

"He's pestering his Grandpa Will."

I finished the bitter liquid. "So, you told him?"

"Remi? Yes. I introduced him to his Grandpa Will and Grandma Hannah."

I wanted asked if she told him I was his papa. My heart thudded, and I held my breath.

"And yes, I told him that Horse Man was his papa. But I'm not sure he understood."

When she scooted closer, I lifted my hand and rested it on her neck as her green eyes held my gaze. I rubbed my thumb on her jawline. She turned her lips toward my hand and kissed it.

"I think it's about time you got up and moved around. Maybe even ate some breakfast."

"You never go easy on me, do you?"

"Not a chance. Come on."

So, I inched toward the edge of the bed. She let me loop my arm over her shoulders and we stood together. I moaned as I tried to place weight on my hurt leg.

"Slow and steady wins this race."

"You're funny."

I hopped toward the kitchen table in the Larson's house. After she held out a chair, I sank into it. Then she rounded to the stove and uncovered a plate, which she set in front of me.

"I'm famished."

Following a quick prayer, I dug in as she watched me eat.

"We're going to stay a few extra days."

I blinked. "We?"

"You, obviously. Me and Remi."

"If you need to head back—"

"It will be nice for Remi to get to know his family. Rio can handle the ranch, and he'll make sure Mama arrives home safely."

Though I hated to keep her from home, I enjoyed the idea of a few more days with her, Remi, and my family. I didn't know when I'd be back. I made enough positive steps to repair relationships with my family, so I welcomed a little more time with them.

"If you're feeling up to it, your mother would really like you at the small ranch house. I think she wants to keep an eye on you to make sure you behave yourself."

"I doubt that. She wants to coddle me and make sure I'm close by so she can help me heal quicker."

Hetty laughed. "She sure knows a lot about medicine."

I told her the story about Mama's first husband, the doctor.

"Oh? Are any of your brothers his?"

I shook my head. "Nope. He passed on the journey west, leaving Mama a widow when she arrived here."

"That must have been hard."

"Not for too long. As she will tell you, Papa stole her heart fairly quickly."

Hetty breathed deeply, then sighed. "They remind me of my parents. So very much in love."

She looked away. "Can I ask you something?"

"'Course."

As she returned her gaze to me, she asked, "Is my papa the one that pulled you from that building?"

I stared into my half full coffee mug and nodded.

"Do you think he recognized you?"

I thought about that for a moment. "I think so."

"I'm glad… He saved you."

My heart squeezed tight. "Even though he died?"

"I wish he hadn't. But I'm glad you came back to me."

As I reached across the table, I held her hand for a minute. "I'm sorry he passed."

Hetty rubbed her thumb on my hand and whispered, "Thank you."

After another heartbeat, she shook off the melancholy and stood.

"Enough lollygagging, Colter. I need to get you over to your mama's house."

"Fine."

When she rounded the table, I pushed the chair away from the table. Then I pulled her onto my lap and wrapped my arms around her waist. She rested her hands behind my neck. I searched her lovely green eyes for a few seconds before I guided her lips toward mine. Then I kissed her sweetly. When she kissed me back, I wrapped my arms around her tightly. I never wanted to let her go. Slowly, I ended the kiss, even though I didn't want to.

"You'll do just about anything to get out of going to your parents' house."

I flashed her one of my roguish grins. "Caught me."

She stood and grabbed my hands. Then she tugged until I stood.

"The house seems far away."

"Remember, slow and steady."

By the time we reached Mama's house, I was exhausted. She directed me to Vi's room, and I flopped onto the bed. Before I knew it, I fell asleep.

Sometime later, I heard laughter from the main room. I pushed myself up and staggered to the door. After I opened it, I leaned against the wall. Papa sat on the floor with Remi, and they played with a toy train.

"Careful," I said. "You might turn him into a railroad man. Wouldn't want him to compete with his uncle."

Hetty laughed. "Not a chance. He comes from a long

line of ranchers. Not sure he has a choice."

I hobbled over to the couch. "I think he can be whatever he sets his mind to."

Hetty sat next to me on the couch and tucked her legs up beside her as she leaned against me.

"Oh, alright. You win."

"That might be a first. Hetty Clark letting me win."

Mama laughed. "You want some coffee or willow bark tea?"

"Coffee's fine."

She brought me a mug and sat in a chair. "He's just the best."

I laughed. "Better than Sterling, Brody, or Jaxson?"

Mama winked at me. "I love all my grandsons equally."

"Uh, huh."

"But Ashley is my favorite granddaughter."

"Unless I lost track over the last few days, she's your only granddaughter."

"For now. I hope for more granddaughters one day."

———

Over the next week, I felt better than the previous day. On my last day, while Papa and Hetty took Remi for a ride, I sat with Mama at the table.

"I'm so glad you came to visit."

"Me too."

During my time on the ranch, something had changed in my relationship with my parents. I no longer questioned their love for me, and I understood them better. Perhaps fa-ther-hood changed my perspective.

Regardless, my love for my parents and my family deep-ened. I committed to writing often, and I hoped we could visit from time to time.

"And thank Hetty for us. For letting us be grandparents to Remi."

"I will."

She set a mug of coffee in front of me.

"The two of you make a good team taking care of Remi."

She glanced down at her mug before she continued. "Do you think you'll marry her?"

I looked out the window. "I want to. My sobriety is a condition for a relationship with her."

Mama patted my hand. "She loves you. When you play with Remi or hold him on your horse, her eyes show it. Soon enough, I think she'll consider it."

My heart ached with hope. The past week solidified my resolve to pursue a life with Hetty. We were a family. Surely, she recognized that.

"Your father and I will pray for the three of you daily."

After the door creaked open, Papa entered the house with Remi balanced on his hip.

"Gam-pa fast horse!" Remi said with ruddy cheeks and a big smile.

"Will." Mama's tone held a warning.

"It was just a trot. Nothing more."

I grinned as Hetty came over and kissed my cheek.

"Of course, I went much faster than a trot. The ranch is so beautiful. So different from the flat prairie land of my place."

"We'll be home tomorrow," I said as I heard the homesickness in her voice. "Thanks for staying with me."

"You'll be alright on a horse and the train tomorrow?"

"I'll be fine." Probably sore and done in by the time we got into her ranch. But it was time to go home.

CHAPTER 19

HETTY

When we reached the top of the hill overlooking Colter Ranch, I waved. My heart ached to leave them behind. In the short time I spent with them, I came to care deeply for Will, Hannah, Sam, and Ellie Mae, and their children. I wondered if I would see them again.

Even though we rode in silence, we arrived at the train station quickly. I was thankful to go home. I missed it.

Once we took our seats on the train and it pulled out of the station, Preston spoke.

"When we're back home, I don't want things to be the same."

As confusion overwhelmed me, my heart pierced. I thought we had bonded during the trip.

"I want to be actively involved in Remi's life. Not just the horse man he visits in the barn."

I let out a slow breath and waited for him to continue.

"Let me be a part of his life. Every evening, I want to spend time with you both. I want to teach him how to ride a horse, rope a steer, and everything else."

The longing for us to be an actual family took deeper

root in my soul. It all sounded so promising if he stayed away from booze.

"I truly want to be his father, Hetty."

"That makes me overjoyed," I whispered. "I think you could start having supper with us and staying after to spend time with him."

Preston cleared his throat. "I don't want to be just his father. I want to be your… I want to court *you*."

A lump lodged in my throat. My pulse raced. Over the last two weeks, things changed between us. My heart had softened toward him. He proved his worth as he became a good father to Remi. When he let go of a lot of pain from his youth, he repaired relationships with his family.

Gone was the wild, rebellious young man. Instead, a grounded, conscientious man appeared. He loved his son. He loved me. Even though he never said the words, it was obvious.

I sighed. He was offering me the next step toward what I always wanted from him.

Yet, in the back of my mind, I doubted his ability to remain sober long term. I would not be tied to a drunk. I'd rather be a single mother than live that life.

As I glanced out the window, my silence made him uncomfortable. I had to think it through. If I ever kicked Preston off my land, I could not extract him from my heart. I already let him get too close to Remi to sever ties with him for good. The connection was already there, and it was strong.

"Alright." I looked at him. "You may court me."

He smiled before he placed a hand on the back of my neck and guided my face closer to his. Then his lips brushed softly against mine. My heart melted like butter on a hot stove. Hopefully, I had not just made the biggest mistake of my life.

When the kiss ended, he slipped his arm around my shoulders and rested the side of his head against the top of mine. We sat that way for a long time with Remi snuggled between us. A genuine family, almost.

Sometime later, Preston nudged me.

"We're here."

I stretched as the train came to a stop.

"You want to get the horses and I'll take Remi?" he asked.

"Yes, that'd be fine."

"We'll wait for you on a bench outside."

When we alighted from the train, I strolled toward the stock car. Our horses were the first off-loaded, so I grabbed their reins and walked toward Preston and Remi.

While I was still a little way off, I spotted John Bartholomew, and he called out to me. I bit the inside of my cheek as I wished I could gracefully ignore him.

"Hetty, I want you to meet someone."

I raised an eyebrow, not expecting that.

"This is my wife, Maud. And her son, Chance."

"Wife?" Guess he finally figured out I was serious when I told him I wouldn't marry him.

"Yes. We met in Prescott. Fell in love and married."

I wasn't sure if I believed the love part. I figured he finally got what he wanted. An heir.

"Congratulations," I said. I smiled at Maud and her son. He looked about eight years old.

"We're your closest neighbors," I added. "Please come for a visit once you get settled. I'm sure my mama, Tildy, would love to meet you."

"John has told me all about you," she said as she smiled sweetly.

Much demurer than me. Good for John. She certainly would suit him better.

"We should talk soon, John, about that parcel, if you're still interested."

"Have your attorney draw up the papers."

We shook hands. Then I bid the new family farewell.

Seemed like John wasted no time solidifying his plans with another woman. Truthfully, I was relieved. One less thing for me to worry about.

"Who was that with John?" Preston asked as he mounted Ranger.

When I held up Remi, he settled our son in his saddle. Then I mounted White Lightning.

"His new wife, Maud. And her son, Chance."

Preston laughed. "Glad to see he didn't pine over you for long."

I smiled and kicked White Lightning into a trot toward home. We arrived at the ranch shortly before suppertime. Preston brought Remi inside. Then he took our horses to the barn.

While I waited for him on the porch, I frowned. He limped slowly from the barn toward the house.

"You feel up to this?" I asked.

"Spending time with my son and my sweetheart? Yeah." Though his smile appeared strained, not quite reaching his eyes.

When he sat at the table, I entered the kitchen and asked Rita to make some willow bark tea for him. Then the four of us shared supper together like a family.

We recounted stories about our last days at Colter Ranch. I told Mama about John Bartholomew. It surprised her, too.

After supper, Preston sat on the floor and played games

with Remi. While I watched them, my heart filled with joy.

"Something is different," Mama said softly from the chair next to me.

"It is. I told Remi that Preston is his papa, and that Will and Hannah were his grandparents."

Mama smiled. "I'm sure they appreciated that."

"Those last few days were special for everyone."

"Something is different between you two."

I let out a long breath. "He told me he wants to be active in Remi's life. He'll be joining us for supper and spending time with us in the evening."

"And?"

I snorted. I never could hide the truth from Mama.

"And he's courting me."

"Your father would be as happy as I am to hear that."

My eyes burned at the mention of Papa. How I missed him. I wondered if he knew he had sacrificed his life for Preston. Perhaps he had done it for me.

"He always hoped you would find your way to each other. He told me many times that he thought Preston was your soulmate."

"Even though we started out all wrong?"

"Yes. That didn't matter to Matt. He knew you well enough to know that your heart chose Preston despite both of your mistakes. We prayed often for both of you."

I turned to look at her.

"I still do, Hetty."

"Thank you, Mama."

We watched as Preston rolled onto his back on the floor and Remi crawled on him. He lifted Remi into the air and lowered him down like he was falling, though Preston's hands held him fast. Remi laughed and smiled.

"He's changed," Mama said. "I can see it clearly."

She meant Preston. I saw it too. I longed to believe the change was permanent. Fear and doubt lingered in the back of my mind, reminding me of how much his abandonment hurt. He could do it again. How I hoped he wouldn't.

I glanced at the clock. "Time for bed, Remi."

Preston sat up. Then he stood and took Remi's hand. "Come on, let's get some shuteye."

Then he took our son back to his bedroom. I joined him and pulled a pair of pajamas from Remi's dresser before I helped Remi change. Then Preston held back the covers as Remi climbed into his bed.

"Story?" Remi asked.

I glanced at Preston. Dark circles buffeted his eyes. He was exhausted.

"Maybe tomorrow night," I said.

"It's alright," Preston said.

"You need some rest. Tomorrow."

He gave in. Then he leaned over and kissed Remi's fore-head. "Good night, son."

My eyes misted.

"Night, horse man."

I'd work with Remi on that.

After I turned down the light, I followed Preston from the room.

CHAPTER 20

PRESTON

It seemed wrong to put my son to bed and then leave the house. I should be there. Ready to help when he woke up. What if he had a nightmare? I sighed. Hetty and Tildy would comfort him like they had for the past two years.

The weariness of travel shrouded me. My footfalls grew heavy as I opened the door.

To my surprise, Hetty slung my arm over her shoulders. She wrapped her arm around my waist and walked with me to the bunkhouse. My leg throbbed fiercely, and her support helped.

Before I reached for the door handle, she led me to a chair on the bunkhouse porch. Then she sat on my lap. I held her close.

"Thank you," she whispered. "I'll work with him about calling you 'Papa'."

"It's alright. A lot has changed. Give him time."

She placed a hand on my cheek, and my heart bucked like that gray mare in Prescott. I pulled her face close to mine, and I kissed her, still holding back from the intensity that I felt. It seemed wise to go slow. As I ended the kiss, I smiled.

"I love you," I said. "Always have. Always will."

Even in the dimming light, I saw her eyes glisten. She cleared her throat and stood.

"I should let you get some rest."

When she tried to walk away, I held her hand for a few breaths.

"Hetty, I mean it. I love you. I love Remi too. We got things all out of order. But that doesn't change my feelings for you both."

She glanced over her shoulder. "I know."

The fear in her eyes was apparent. I didn't push, but released her hand and let her go.

"Night!" I called after her. She waved a hand in the air as she continued back to her house.

———

The days turned to weeks. My leg healed fully. My evenings filled me with joy and happiness as I ate with my family—that's what Hetty, Remi, and Tildy were to me. Not officially. Not yet. But that didn't matter to my heart and my soul. They were my family. My life.

As I dismounted Ranger in front of the Caldwell home, I took a deep breath. I hoped I could prove myself worthy of a life with Hetty.

"Deep in thought already?" Rich asked as he walked past me.

After I tied Ranger to the post, I sighed loudly.

"Something wrong with Hetty?"

"No. Lots of things are right," I answered.

He held the door of the house open for me. "Then why the dark cloud?"

"I told you we're courting."

He nodded.

Iris paused next to me as she held her lunch plate. "Are you? What have you done besides dine at her table and sit next to her in church?"

I blinked.

Iris put one hand on her hip. "That's what I thought. You aren't courting Hetty at all. You're playing parent to your son and doing a good job of that. But you most definitely are not courting your son's mother."

Clyde stood next to his wife with drawn eyebrows.

"I'm leaving now," she said. "I said what needed to be said."

With that, she hurried out to the front porch.

"She has a point," Brian said. "If Remi wasn't in the picture, would you call what you're doing courting?"

Slowly, I shook my head as I sat in a chair. Iris already set plates of sandwiches at each of our seats.

Thomas entered the house out of breath. "Sorry, I'm late. We had an urgent issue at the train station this morning."

After Clyde blessed our meal, Thomas asked, "What did I miss?"

"Just Iris scolding Preston," Rich said under his breath.

Thomas turned wide eyes toward me. "What did you do?"

"That's the problem," Brian interjected before I could think up a response. "He's not really courting Hetty, and Iris called him out on it."

"I thought Iris wasn't supposed to get involved," I mutter-ed.

Clyde laughed. "With Hetty Clark, it's hard to stop her. She has a sweet spot for her, like an overprotective aunt."

I frowned. "Please tell me she's not related."

"She's not. She just cares for her like she is."

I sighed. "So, now that we have figured out my problem, what do I do about it?"

"Flowers!" Iris yelled from the front porch.

I pointed to the front porch and turned up my palms, hoping Clyde would do something about it.

"She doesn't normally listen in, does she?" Brian asked.

"No. I can assure you she doesn't." Clyde stood and closed the front door. "She is right. You should take her some flowers today."

"Maybe buy her a gift. Plan a date," Thomas said.

"Just the two of you," Rich added.

I wondered when my posse became such romantics.

"The new hotel is open," Thomas said. "And they have a wonderful restaurant. The passengers at the train station speak highly about it."

"You could take her for dinner. Shoot, she might wear a dress for that," Rich said.

I snorted. "Let's not get too crazy."

Even though the conversation moved on from me, I took what they said to heart. They were right. Iris was right. Since coming back from Prescott, all my time with Hetty centered around time with our son. Other than a few stolen kisses, we spent no time alone together.

When our meeting finished, Iris entered the house before we all left.

"My rose garden is blooming nicely. I picked a few blooms for you."

I chuckled. "You mean for Hetty."

"From you," Iris said coyly as she finished snipping off the thorns. She handed them to me.

"Thank you for looking out for us."

I said my farewell and headed back to the ranch with

flowers in hand. Maybe a picnic was the answer.

As I neared the ranch, I saw Hetty walking to the house from the barn. I pulled Ranger to a stop by the house. Then I tied him to the post. I knocked on the door before opening it.

"Hello!" I called out.

Tildy sat in the parlor reading a book. "She just went into her office," she said without looking up. When she did, she let out an 'oh'. Then gave me a knowing smile.

I nodded a greeting and proceeded to Hetty's office.

"Afternoon," I said as I hid the roses behind my back.

Hetty shuffled some papers for a few seconds before she looked up. She smiled. "Come on in."

I rounded her desk to stand close to her. Then I held out the roses. "For you."

Her cheeks turned pink, and she bit her lower lip.

"Um… Thank you." She took the flowers from my hand. "How was your meeting?"

"Good."

When Hetty said nothing, I went to search for something for the flowers. Once I found Rita, she handed me a vase with some water.

"Muy bueno," she said as she patted my arm and smiled.

After I returned to Hetty's office, I set the vase on the corner of her desk. She stood and placed the roses in the water.

"They are lovely."

Then I removed my hat and held it in my hands. "I was wonder-ing… Would you like to have a picnic with me on Saturday?"

She smiled softly, and her eyes glinted. "That would be fun. I'm sure Remi would like that."

I shook my head. "Just you and me."

Her hand rested on her neck. "Oh. Um… Yes."

"I gotta go take care of Ranger. See you for supper."

"Hmm. Right."

I smiled as I backed away, leaving Hetty speechless. It was a first. I would have to thank Iris on Sunday.

CHAPTER 21

HETTY

When I woke up on Saturday, I touched the petals of the roses. Last night, I placed the vase in my bedroom so I could enjoy the flowers first thing. I still couldn't believe Preston had brought me flowers.

Slowly, I stretched and rose from the bed. Then I leaned over the flowers and breathed in their heady fragrance as excitement bubbled up inside me.

A picnic. Just us. We'd never done that.

I paced the length of my room as my heart stuttered. I stood before my wardrobe and glanced at the three dresses hanging there. They were nothing fancy. Practical, like me. For the first time, I wished I owned a fancy dress that made me feel feminine.

As I closed my eyes, I let out a slow breath. Then I opened them again. I had never wished for a fancy dress before. I wasn't a fancy dress woman.

I closed the wardrobe and pulled out a pair of tan trousers and a solid blue button-down shirt. Yup. Plain and practical, like me.

After brushing out my hair, I braided it and flicked it over my shoulder. Best to be myself for my picnic outing with Preston.

When I entered the dining room, I kissed Remi on the cheek, thankful that Mama dressed him this morning.

Mama snorted when she saw me. "You gonna change be-fore your picnic date?"

I frowned, and doubt filled my heart. "Wasn't planning on it."

Mama raised an eyebrow and said nothing more.

Perhaps Preston would like me to wear a dress. I shook my head. No. He knew that wasn't me. I only wore dresses on Sunday.

"Buenos días, señorita," Rita said. "When is your picnic with Preston?"

"Around lunchtime I figure."

"I'll have a picnic basket ready for you by eleven."

"Thank you, Rita."

As soon as breakfast finished, I stepped onto the porch. When I saw White Lightning tied to the post, I stopped short. I looked around and saw no one, so I untied him. There was a note conspicuously tucked under the edge of his saddle. I unfolded it.

Morning, my sweet Hetty. Looking forward to our picnic outing. See you when you return.

Heat warmed my cheeks as I stuffed the note in my pocket. I mounted White Lightning and raced toward the herd. Once I neared, I veered off to ride the fence line. When I finished inspecting the fence, I turned back toward the herd and spoke with Rio for several minutes.

"Señorita, you don't want to be late for your picnic. Vete!" He motioned me away with his hands.

I sighed. It seemed the whole ranch knew about our date.

By the time I returned to the house, Preston waited for me. I took a minute to study him as his shoulder leaned against the porch railing. One leg crossed over the other with the toe of his boot propped on the ground. His lips stretched in a grin, showing his white teeth. He straightened when he saw me. My, he looked handsome.

"Ready?"

I hesitated as I considered running into the house to change into a dress. I let out a quiet breath and nodded before Preston smoothly mounted Ranger. My eyes locked with his stunning blue ones for a few heartbeats.

"You look—"

"Plain? Practical?"

He frowned. "Why would you say that?"

I sighed. "Mama thinks I should have worn a dress."

The corner of his eyes crinkled with unspoken laughter. "I might not have recognized you if you did."

Rolling my eyes, I smirked.

"Come on, let's go. We've got a bit of a ride to the spot I picked out."

He kicked Ranger into a trot. When I caught up to him, he slowed to a walk.

"Are you happy here?" I asked.

"Very much."

"Content to be a wrangler?"

He glanced at me. "I dream of becoming more than a wrangler."

My heart skipped a beat as his eyes connected with mine. I looked away, since I was not ready to talk about our relationship yet.

Preston cleared his throat. "I thought, if you let me stick

around, I could build a horse breeding and training business for us."

Us. My breath shallowed and flutters danced in my middle. I wanted there to be an 'us'. A happily ever after. If only I believed he wouldn't leave me again and that he'd stay sober forever.

My eyes burned as the rejection from my past fought its way forward to my present. I kicked White Lightning into a gallop along the same trajectory we'd been traveling. As the wind burned my face, the tears fell. The pain felt as fresh as two years ago.

Before the landscape changed from the flat plains to a trail along a canyon wall, I pulled my horse to a stop. I swiped at the moisture on my face. Sobs that I stuffed down years ago rose to the surface. The ache in my gut stole the air from my lungs and I slid off White Lightning as I dropped to my knees.

"Hetty!"

Ranger skidded to a stop next to White Lightning. Preston lifted me to my feet and pulled me close.

"What's wrong?"

His voice reverberated through his chest to my ear. I lost all control and held onto his middle as if he might vanish any second.

"Shh. It's alright, my love."

Warm hands caressed my hair while I struggled to regain control.

"I love you, Preston. And I hate you. You left me when I needed you. Remi needed you."

I pushed back from his arms and forced some space between us before I leaned down to pick up my hat from the ground. After I brushed the dust from it, I slammed it down on my head. Ire. It would help me through this tangled mess of emotions.

As I took a step forward, I looked into his eyes. I poked a finger in his chest.

"How can I trust you again? You left. You rejected me and left me. Yet, you command this part of my heart that I can't regain control of. It's yours. It always has been and always will be."

Preston said nothing, but reached for my arms.

"These last few weeks give me hope." I brushed his hands away. "But how do I know you won't leave me and Remi? How do I know something won't drive you back to the bottle? How can I really trust you? Us?"

He looked away. "You can't know for sure. If you could, it wouldn't be called trust."

When he turned to face me, he took another step closer. This time, I didn't move away. I let him hold my arms.

"I'm trying, Hetty. Harder than I've tried anything before." He snorted. "Riding a bronc seems easier than trying to win your trust again. I hurt you and was selfish. I know I don't deserve you. Or Remi."

He coughed. "I don't deserve to be a part of your family or to become your husband or Remi's father. But it's what I want. And I will do whatever you ask me to in order to make it happen because I love you both."

The air between us heated as I studied his eyes. I saw so much. Desire, regret, hurt, love. Then pleading and finally hope.

Hope. I wanted to give into it. I wanted to believe this time would be different. That I could trust him with my heart.

"I can't promise I won't hurt you again. I'm far too flawed to promise that." He leaned down to eye level with me. "I am committed to staying sober. As much as I wish I could promise I'll never fail, I can't. I may. But I don't want to. I want, no, I pray I will remain a new man—a man who will one day be worthy of your trust."

My eyes darted away from his intense stare. I took a deep breath and closed my eyes. Then I let it out slowly.

"I'm trying too. It's hard to let go of the hurt. I'm trying to place my trust in you again."

"Look at me."

I did.

"That's all I could ask for."

Then his fingers brushed lightly across my cheek. "Shall we continue on to our picnic?"

I nodded. "Thank you."

We mounted our horses again. Then he led us into the ravine to a beautiful spot near the flowing stream. There was a flat dirt area next to a rock God made specifically to hold a picnic lunch.

"Rio mentioned this place," he said. "He and Rita like to come here. They've even brought Remi a few times. He said your parents liked the spot as well."

After I dismounted, he tied both our horses nearby. Then he shook out a blanket near the rock and laid it on the ground. A cluster of tall trees cast shade over the area.

As he set out the lunch, I sat on the blanket. Then he sat next to me. Warmth spread through my middle as he blessed the meal. Then he handed me a sandwich. I took a bite as my eyes traveled over the scene before us.

The stream gurgled as it weaved through trees and brush. The proximity of the water and the shade of the junipers guarding us cooled the bright sun's warmth. I closed my eyes and allowed peace to seep deep into my soul.

When I opened my eyes again, I noticed a family of quail scurried across the path further downstream. A distant dream danced before my eyes. Me, Preston, Remi, and siblings for Remi. I laughed and joy filled my soul.

As I blinked, the image vanished, replaced by the swift stream. I took another bite of my sandwich and swallowed it.

"Tell me about the horse business," I said.

"Back before… Anyway, I used to work at my uncle's stables. He bred and trained horses. Larson Stables. You may have heard of it."

"I have. Purchased a horse or two from him."

"I learned everything I know about horses from Uncle Adam. I love working with horses. Clark Stables has a nice ring, don't you think?"

My breath caught. "Not Colter?"

"Not hardly. I have no money to invest in the idea. So, my investor's name would go on the business. If you want to invest in it."

We finished eating, and he slid his arm around me. I leaned into his side and breathed deeply. He smelled of hay and spice.

"I have the money from the parcel that John bought. Been saving it for a rainy day."

"Then you should hold on to it."

"Not so fast. Let's look at the numbers later. See if it makes sense."

I snuggled closer to him. "For now, I'd like to enjoy the time with my beau."

He laughed. "You asked."

"I know. And now I'm done talking business."

"Alright. What would you like to talk about?"

I angled my head up to meet his gaze and smiled. "Maybe I'm not that interested in talking."

The look in his eyes—I barely registered it before his lips

captured mine. He leaned down on the blanket and pulled me along with him. When he deepened the kiss and lodged his hand in my hair, I moaned and returned his kiss. I missed him when we were apart. Longing overwhelmed me as he gently guided me to my back. His lips warmed my neck as his hands caressed my side.

"Preston." The desire in my voice told the truth even as I pushed him away. "We shouldn't."

His hands froze as his breaths came quickly. Ever so slowly, he sat up on the blanket and distanced himself from me. A saucy grin spread across his mouth.

"If we were married, there would be no 'shouldn'ts'."

He held his hand out to help me up.

"You're evil."

He laughed. "Some things aren't likely to change."

Once he stood, he packed up lunch, still grinning like the rogue he was.

"Come on. Let's get you home before Rio sends out the search party."

I laughed as I mounted White Lightning, and we headed home as my heart filled with joy.

CHAPTER 22

September 10, 1893

HETTY

A month had passed since my picnic date with Preston. Once a week, we took an afternoon or evening just for us. One of those dates was a nice dinner in town at the hotel. I even wore a dress. When I stepped from the house in a dress, his face screwed up. He acted like he didn't believe it was me. Later, he told me how beautiful I looked and I enjoyed it.

Remi's birthday arrived and brought with it another milestone. Two years ago, I labored long into the night until dawn broke the next morning to bring my sweet, fatherless son into the world. Mama and Rita helped me. According to Mama, Papa paced in the living room the entire night, praying for me. Then it was over.

My little Remington Matthew Clark cooed in my arms. His blue eyes instantly reminded me of Preston. The sadness of his rejection didn't last long. Remi's hunger took precedence over my sorrow. Love quickly replaced it as my perfect son became my priority and focus.

Despite the whispers from snobbish gossipers in town, I held my head high week after week when I entered the church. In time, the whispers faded. The only people who knew about Remi's father, besides my parents, were Rio, Rita, Clyde, and Iris. They never shamed me or treated me differently because of my mistake. Instead, Iris showed me kind-ness. Many times in the earliest days, she came to help with Remi to give me and Mama a break.

"Why the distant look?" Preston asked as he entered the house after he cared for the horses following church.

"Just remembering Remi's arrival."

He leaned down and placed a kiss on my cheek. A quiet yelp came from his shirt.

"What—?"

Preston reached inside his shirt and pulled out a fluffy brown puppy. He grinned. "I couldn't help myself. Rich told me about a client that had a few weened puppies. A boy needs a friend, and I thought…"

I raised an eyebrow. "He's only two. He can't care for a dog."

"I'll take care of her."

I snorted. "What if she needs let out in the middle of the night?"

Preston's smile faded, and my heart ached to crush his hopes. "Do you want me to keep her at the bunkhouse?"

"Puppy!" Remi squealed, cutting off any further discussion.

When Preston hesitated, I nodded. Then he leaned down and gave the puppy to our son.

"We need to pick a name for her," he said.

Remi hugged the brown ball of fur next to his chest. "Soft!"

I smiled. Guess we'd figure out how to take care of her,

because there was no taking her back from my son.

Preston showed Remi the proper way to handle a dog. Then he suggested some names.

"Brownie?"

Remi shook his head.

"Molasses?"

Another head shake.

"Brandy?"

Remi giggled.

Preston looked at me.

"I guess her name is Brandy," I said.

Rita called us to the dining room. Remi walked into the room and Brandy followed behind him. When Remi tried to pick her up, I stopped him.

"She stays on the floor."

Remi pouted, so Preston distracted him, then he showed Brandy where to lie. She laid down and stared at Remi for the entire meal.

After we finished eating, we celebrated Remi's birthday with cake before we adjourned to the living room.

When I sat down on the couch, Preston sat next to me. He looped an arm around my shoulder as we watched Remi play with Brandy. I decided I'd wait to give him his new hat later. My son was too enamored with the puppy.

"I'm sorry," Preston whispered in my ear.

"Oh, it's alright. Clearly, he loves her already."

"No. I'm sorry I wasn't there for you. I'm sorry I missed his birth."

I sniffed and bit my lip, trying to get my emotions under control.

Preston said nothing else. Instead, he rubbed the base of my neck, never taking his eyes off Remi or Brandy. When Brandy started to squat, Preston shot to his feet and grabbed her.

"No!" Remi screamed.

After I picked up Remi, we followed Preston out of the house.

"She has to go potty," he explained. "We take her outside when she has to go."

Remi calmed, so I set him down. He watched as Brandy took care of her business in the yard. When she bounded up the porch stairs, Remi squealed.

"Good," he said as he patted Brandy's head. Then the pair moseyed into the house.

I stayed on the front porch. Once Preston closed the door to the house, he remained with me.

After a deep breath, I let it out slowly. He stood behind me and wrapped his arms around me. Then I rested my head against his chest.

"You are a good father," I whispered.

He snorted.

"I mean it. You are good with him. You probably don't even realize it, but every time you interact with him, you teach him things. It seems so natural, the way you do it."

He cleared his throat. "It's what I remember my father doing."

"Like my papa, yours is a good man, too."

"Better man than I've been."

A sudden urge to defend him rose inside me. "You are a good man."

He said nothing. Instead, he rubbed his hand on my arm.

"You are the reason Remi is such a good boy," he said. "You balance instruction with love and wisdom."

He cleared his throat. "You remind me of my mother. You teach without words. Your entire life is the lesson."

I thought about his mother, Hannah. She welcomed me into her home, even though she suspected my son was Preston's—born outside of marriage. She never made me feel judged or condemned. I could see what Preston met.

"Tell me," I said. Then I faced him. "With such amazing parents, what happened to you?"

He moved away from me and grasped the porch railing with both hands.

"I always felt like no one saw me. I didn't matter. I was a fifth son. Not much to offer. Certainly not with four perfect sons going before me."

I rubbed a hand on his back and listened.

"I never measured up to any of them. James was smarter than me. Sam was better with numbers. Boone was wild and rowdy, but great at everything he ever tried. Then there was Deacon. He was the smartest of us all. He saw things no one else would imagine."

As I wrapped my arms around his waist, I rested my cheek against his back.

"I was only good with horses."

"But your parents loved you. That was obvious when we were at their ranch."

"I see that now. Unfortunately, I couldn't see that then. I was always the sensitive one. Boone decided it was his job to toughen me up. Instead, it made me feel broken."

I rubbed my hand over his arm that settled over mine.

"I didn't know what to do with those feelings. I went to a dark, destructive place. With the help of my posse, I'm learn--ing how to change that."

"Walk with me?" I asked.

He took my hand in his as we stepped off the porch. I still wore my dress from church, so I lifted the hem so as not to trip on it as we walked over the uneven ground between the house and the barn.

Once we arrived in the barn, I leaned against the wall. Then I pulled him to me.

"I'm glad you came back into my life," I said as I placed a hand on his cheek. "I love you. I love watching you with our son. I think—"

"Hetty!"

The fear in Mama's voice ended our conversation. I ran out of the barn to catch up to her on the path.

"Is Remi with you?"

I shook my head as horror settled into the pit of my stomach.

"Rita and I can't find him or Brandy anywhere."

With wide eyes, I looked at Preston.

"We searched the house. They aren't there. We don't see them walking toward the pastures."

Preston frowned. "Let's look for tracks near the house."

While we walked back toward the house, I hung my head low as my eyes scanned the dirt for any sign of puppy paw prints or Remi's little boot tracks. Nothing. We walked around to the back of the house.

"Here." Preston pointed to some depressions in the dirt.

Then his face went pale. "Might be headed toward the picnic spot."

I glanced up at the sky as dusk settled over the ranch. My son disappeared and night stalked us. I ran toward the barn, but Preston caught my wrist.

"Hetty."

I tried to wrench my arm free, but he held it tight.

"We'll never find him in the dark. There's no moon tonight. Nothing to be done until morning."

"I have to find him."

Preston pulled me close. His arms gripped me despite

my attempts to struggle free.

My son was alone in the wilderness. Coyotes. Snakes. Many dangers surrounded him. I had to go.

CHAPTER 23

PRESTON

As I rode into town, Hetty's wails still rang in my ears. Night nipped at my heels when I arrived to the glow of light from a few saloons and businesses.

My heart broke. My son was missing. The woman I loved hated me. She had to. If I hadn't bought Remi that puppy, he would have had no reason to go outside. This was all my fault.

The tinny sound of the music from the saloon snagged my attention for a moment. Couldn't do anything to help my son that night. It'd be so easy to turn right and tie Ranger in front of the saloon. Just one drink. It would ease my fear and help me sleep.

No. One drink would turn to two. I would lose both Remi and Hetty if I did that.

Still, it would be easier to find my son the next morning if I got a good night's sleep.

No. I was there for Clyde. Rich. Brian. Thomas.

I turned Ranger toward the livery. Once there, I knocked on the door.

"Preston. What's going on?"

"Remi is missing. We must ride out at first light to find him."

"Whoa, hold up. What do you mean, Remi is missing?"

"He took off with that puppy. We think he might have gone toward a picnic spot near a ravine."

I grabbed Rich's shirt and shook him. "We have to find him!"

Rich shoved me back, and I released his shirt. He grabbed my arm and pulled me into his house.

"Tell me everything," he said as he pointed toward a chair at the table. Then he set a coffee in front of me.

After I took a sip, I told him the story. How I gave Remi the puppy and showed him we had to take her outside to go potty.

"That has to be why he left. He's never done something like that before."

Several minutes passed. Rich finally suggested we pray.

Once I calmed down, he left and got Thomas and Brian. Thomas suggested I wire down to my family to let them know to pray. It seemed like an odd thing to wire to someone. But I gave him the money, and he sent the telegram.

When he returned, Clyde came with him. The four of us prayed through the night for my son and for Hetty.

As soon as the first hint of daylight arrived, we saddled up and headed toward the ranch. Iris provided food for our saddlebags so we could head out to the ravine to look for him without going all the way to the ranch.

A flash of a rider flew past me on a black stallion. White cowboy hat. Red beard. If I didn't know better, I'd think it was Boone.

Then the rider wheeled around toward me.

I blinked.

"Preston. I'm here. Tell me what you know."

It *was* Boone. My brother. The one who tormented me as a young man. He sat on top of his horse, Outlaw. His blue eyes flashed with fire.

"We got your telegram," Boone explained. "I went to James's Superintendent of Transportation's home right away and got him to find me a spot on the overnight freight train. His name's Daniel Parker. I know him from the construction we've done on the line. He sent the word out to Papa and Mama. They're praying."

As I rubbed my eyes, my head tilted to the side. Boone was here.

"I'm an excellent tracker. You know I can find anything. Let's go. Show me the tracks you found."

I nodded numbly and kicked Ranger into a gallop back to the ranch. Boone kept pace with me. Boone.

We dismounted, and I showed him. He crouched down and walked toward the tracks. I thought the tracks had disappeared, but Boone walked further and found where they picked up again.

"This way!"

In a matter of seconds, he was back on his horse. His eyes never left the ground as he led the way. My posse and I followed. Hetty pulled up next to me on her horse.

"When did he get here?"

I shook my head. "Over night, I guess."

Still couldn't believe my big brother came to help.

"How did he know to come?"

"I sent a telegram to my parents to pray. They must have delivered it to him instead. I don't exactly know. I'm just glad he's here. He can follow a trail better than most. The outdoors is his domain."

"I was gonna ride out to the picnic spot," she said.

I watched as Boone followed tracks to the northeast.

The picnic spot was due west.

As I shook my head, I said, "Don't go. I don't think he's there."

She frowned. "I have to do something."

My mind rolled through all the horrific possibilities of what we might find. A coyote could have mauled him. Bitten by a rattlesnake. Kid-napped by rustlers. Trampled by cattle. It would kill her to see his dead body. I had to spare her from the sight.

"Go home. Let me find him."

When I reached for her, she turned White Lightning in a circle. "He's my son."

"Please, Hetty. Just this once, do as I ask."

She narrowed her eyes and scanned my face. Tears brimmed in her eyes.

"I will bring him back to you. I promise." Knowing I shouldn't make a promise like that, I choked on the words.

After a few more seconds, she turned her horse back toward the ranch and galloped home.

I wasted no time. When I kicked Ranger to a trot, we quickly caught up to Boone.

My brother had his field glasses out and surveyed the barren horizon. Tall grass covered the land, broken up sporadically by short ironwood trees and scrub brush. Surely, if Remi was out there, we'd be able to see him.

Lord, please help us find him. Alive.

Boone stood in his stirrups and leaned forward. Then he stowed his field glasses and galloped toward a distant spot. Rich, Brian, Thomas, and Clyde followed behind. I kicked Ranger for his best speed until I caught up with my brother.

Once I was parallel to him, he pointed toward an ironwood tree. A lump of bright blue rested beneath it. I choked on the emotion filling my throat. As I clamped my jaw tight, I pushed Ranger to the front.

Time seemed to slow the faster we rode. Thundering hooves sounded all around me. The blue blob grew bigger the closer we came. Then a round, furry brown spot wiggled its butt.

Brandy. She tried to make herself look bigger as she barked. Then she turned to the blue lump. Slowly, it moved.

I finally breathed.

She licked his face, and he sat up.

At last, we reached him. I yanked back hard on Ranger's reins, so much he reared up. I slid off his back and left him there while I ran to my son.

Within seconds, I scooped him up into my arms and cried. Not the crying a woman does. No, it was the dry tears that come from a father's loving heart when he's reunited with his lost son.

"Papa!" Remi cried.

My heart lodged in my throat as my son's tears wet his face. I rocked him back and forth while Brandy pawed at my leg and licked my pants.

"Shh. I've got you. You're safe."

His little shoulders shook as I held him slightly away from me. A scratch ran down the side of his cheek. Dirt streaked his forehead. His blue eyes that matched mine were rimmed in red. And he looked perfect.

I pulled him close to my chest as a brawny hand clamped down on my shoulder. When I glanced up, I saw moisture in the corner of Boone's eyes before he sniffed and turned away.

For another minute, I sat there holding my son. Clyde's lips moved as his head bowed. Rich helped me up as I clutched Remi close. Brian leaned down and scooped up Brandy. She squirmed in his arms until he let her sniff Remi.

Then she calmed. Thomas hugged me, careful not to squish my son.

My posse and my brother came through for me. I never would have found Remi without them. Or without God.

"Praise God!" Brian yelled.

His grin became infectious. Soon all of us beamed. Boone wrapped his arm around my shoulders and squeezed me against his side. Then he held Remi while I mounted Ranger. Boone smoothed out Remi's hair before he handed him up to me.

Once my son settled against me, he dozed off. Brian handed Boone the puppy. Then my posse rode toward town, while the rest of us rode toward the ranch.

As the adrenaline faded, I let out a shaky breath.

"You alright?" Boone asked.

I cleared my throat. "Thank you for coming. For… Finding him."

When I looked at him, Boone's throat worked.

"How did you end up with the telegram?"

He coughed. "God. There's no other explanation for it. Someone clearly addressed the telegram to Papa. No idea why they delivered it to my home."

My gaze dropped to the top of my son's head. "Why did you come?"

Boone cleared his throat. "I'm a father, Preston. All I could think about was if Jaxson was lost."

He shifted in his saddle. Then he laughed. "And I know what a terrible tracker you are."

He winked as I looked at him. I snorted. "I am, aren't I?"

"You are."

When his smile faded, he readjusted Brandy. "Besides, you're my brother. For something like this, I will always be here for you."

Emotion welled up in my chest.

"I mean it, brother. We're Colters. I will always have your back."

We grew silent for several minutes.

At last, I said, "Thank you."

In the distance, I recognized a pinto. Sam? And a broad-shouldered man rode next to him on a brown horse.

"Is that…?"

Boone laughed. "Sam and Deacon. Don't know how they made it here."

My brothers came.

"Of course, they waited until I did all the hard work." Boone's laughter rang across the pasture.

Whatever negative feelings I had toward him vanished. He came through for me when it mattered the most. I loved him and all my brothers. And I vowed never again would I doubt they loved me.

CHAPTER 24

HETTY

"Hetty, calm down," Mama said.

"How can you say that? Remi is missing."

"Preston will find him."

When Mav burst through the front door, I jumped.

"Riders."

I pushed past him and ran out the door. When I didn't recognize the horses, I stopped short. Mama stood next to me.

"Who...?"

As they rode closer, I recognized Will and Hannah Colter. Deacon? Sam?

The lump in my throat made it difficult to speak. Once the men dismounted, Deacon reached up and helped his mother off her horse. She let out a sigh when her feet touched the ground.

"How?" I squeaked. The morning train from Prescott wouldn't arrive for another two hours.

Hannah rubbed her back as she climbed the porch stairs. Then she drew me into her arms.

When she released me, she said, "James owns a railroad."

"Mama, he's only a part owner," Deacon said.

She waved her hand in the air. "Just before dawn, we hopped in his private car."

"Daniel Parker, one of James's men arranged it," Will said. "James is still in Chicago."

"We brought a stock car for the horses, too," Deacon said.

"Tell us how we can help," Sam said.

"I… I.."

"Come on in," Mama said. "Rita! We have guests."

Deacon and Sam stayed outside while Will and Hannah joined us inside. A few minutes later, I heard Deacon and Sam ride off.

"Deacon must have found tracks," Will said as he sat at the table.

I sank into a chair. Preston's family came. I shook my head as I sipped my coffee.

"Vi wanted to come too," Hannah said. "But we sent her off to school. Not much she could have done to help, anyway."

My anxiety settled. Just their presence seemed to soothe my fractured nerves.

"More riders!" Mav hollered from the front door.

I shot to my feet so fast that the chair toppled over. I heard someone set it upright as I ran through the door.

Four brothers rode side by side. My eyes darted to the liver chestnut and my man. Then I spotted my son.

"Remi!" His name tore from my throat in a strangled yell.

My feet flew to Preston as he pulled Ranger to a stop. Then he handed Remi to me. I held my son close, and sobs shook my body. Preston's comforting arms wrapped around us both.

"Mama." Remi's voice muffled against my shirt. He sniffed. "Papa find."

My head snapped up as I searched Preston's eyes.

He cleared his throat. "Yes, son. Papa and Uncle Boone found you."

Then he whispered in my ear, "I keep my promises."

As my heart squeezed tighter, I buried my head against his chest. When Remi squirmed, I set him down.

"Mimi!"

Once I was certain Mama held him, I clutched Preston. "Thank you."

His hand stroked my hair as his other arm held me close. When the surrounding noise quieted, I lifted my head. His eyes searched mine for a few seconds before his lips consumed mine. My hands roamed over his back as one of his caressed my neck. The other pressed my low back hard against him. Fire coursed through my body, and I expressed my gratitude and longing with the kiss.

When he groaned, he abruptly released me and stepped back.

"Marry me, Hetty."

My chest heaved as my breaths came in spurts. I wrapped my arms around my middle and looked toward the barn.

Preston grabbed my arms. "Please. Let us be the family we're meant to be. Let me be your husband."

I glanced at him as the old fears clawed their way to the surface. Then I looked away.

"I'm begging you."

When I turned away from him, his hands released me.

"I... Now is not the time."

As I glanced over my shoulder, I watched his slump. He untied the horses and led them to the barn. Tears blurred my vision as I entered the house. Deacon walked past me, along with Will.

Fear wrapped around my heart and crushed the life from it. I wasn't ready to marry Preston. Not even after he found my son. I had to be as crazy as a loon.

———

PRESTON

My heart died within my chest over Hetty's rejection. Any joy I felt about my family's presence disappeared in the darkness, swallowing me whole.

As I led Ranger into his stall, I went through the motions. Take off the saddle. Brush him down.

I dropped my forehead on his back and let my arms hang limp at my sides. I felt dead inside.

A familiar, warm hand squeezed my shoulder. Without looking, I knew it was Papa.

"She won't marry me."

He took the brush from my hand. Then he ran it along Ranger's back and side. I slunk away from my horse and leaned against the wall before I crossed my arms over my chest.

Papa glanced up at me but said nothing. His dark eyes studied me. His expression grim.

"Maybe I should come… Home."

A frown flickered across his face. "This is your home, isn't it?"

"Is it? If Hetty won't marry me, then why am I here?"

Papa cleared his throat. "For your son."

"I can't. I can't keep pretending to be a family. She clearly doesn't want me."

His hand stopped for a few seconds before he resumed brushing my horse.

"It hurts too much."

I stepped closer to Ranger and rubbed his muzzle.

"I promised to bring Remi home. I did. And still, she refuses to trust me. How can I prove myself?"

Papa shook his head. "I don't know, son."

He came around and squeezed my shoulder.

"I'm tired," I said. "I'm going to my bunk. Fetch me for supper."

Then I turned and hurried out of the barn as the darkness in my soul enveloped me.

CHAPTER 25

PRESTON

If my family hadn't been visiting, I would have eaten supper in the bunkhouse. Instead, I trudged over to the main house for the meal. When I arrived, my mama hugged me, and my brothers greeted me.

When I looked around, Hetty was gone. So was Remi. Tildy told me they were sleeping before she invited us into the dining room.

We all sat down at the table. Tildy offered a blessing full of gratitude for finding Remi. Once she finished, we passed food around the table.

"After supper, we must go back to town," Mama said. "We're staying at the hotel."

"We have a room here," Tildy said. "And some bunks in the bunkhouse."

"Thank you for your hospitality, but we won't impose," Papa said. "We're scheduled to leave for Prescott first thing."

Mama rubbed her back again. She must be sore from the horse ride. She rarely rode. Didn't even have her own horse. It was Ellie Mae's horse she came in on.

Guilt tugged at my heart.

"Mama, I'll hitch up the carriage and drive you in. I'll stay with Rich and come back in the morning."

"Bless you," Mama said as she squeezed my hand. "I'm not accustomed to riding so much."

During the rest of the meal, I said little. Remi woke as Rita cleared the plates. So, I held him while he ate. Brandy laid under my chair.

When he finished, my parents played with him in the parlor until Deacon and I brought the carriage and horses around. Then they said their farewells.

I drove the carriage with Mama next to me.

"Tell me, what are you thinking?" she asked.

After I cleared my throat, I said, "I'm thinking about coming back to the ranch. Colter Ranch."

When she looped her hand around my arm, I found it comforting.

"It's too hard to live here. Acting like a family and knowing we never will be."

"You've given up hope, then?"

Her words sliced through my dead heart as I nodded.

Mama patted my arm. "Though we'd love to have you, I think you should stay here. If not at Clark Ranch, then in town."

"Why?"

"Your son is here. Even if Hetty never... Surely, the two of you can arrange a schedule for you to visit him. Tildy would make sure that happens."

My eyes studied my papa's back as he rode ahead of us. I remembered what he said in July about weighing the consequences of drinking. He didn't want to lose his wife and children. Neither did I.

Only Hetty wasn't my wife. No matter how hard I tried, she refused my proposal. I doubted if her heart would ever budge.

But Mama was right. I wanted to be Remi's father. If I lived in Prescott, I'd never see him.

"Can you find a job in town?" Mama asked, pulling me out of my thoughts.

"I don't know."

I glanced at her and she gave me her full attention.

"I've been thinking about starting a horse breeding and training business. There's a lot of opportunity here. We're close to some enormous ranches."

"So why not do that?"

As I shook my head, my face heated. "I don't have the money."

"Ask your uncle."

"Pardon?"

"Ask Adam. He's talked about wanting to expand for years. We don't have the property to support it. He and Julia even considered moving to their own land. Perhaps, instead of them leaving Colter Ranch, he'd be open to investing in a second Larson Stables. One in Ash Fork."

A dim flicker of hope sparked in my soul. Then it grew as I considered it.

"Mama, you are brilliant."

She laughed. "James isn't the only entrepreneur in the family."

I hugged her to my side as the plan formed in my mind. Then I kissed the top of her head.

"That's perfect. Thank you, Mama."

Once we arrived in Ash Fork, I turned around and headed back to Clark Ranch. In the morning, I'd take Ranger and my meager belongings and head back to Colter Ranch with my family. I needed to meet with Uncle Adam as soon as possible to set things in motion.

———

HETTY

"What do you mean, you're leaving?" I asked with my hands propped on my hips.

My throat constricted. Preston was abandoning us again, just like I knew he would.

"Just for a few weeks. Then I'll be close by, in Ash Fork."

I frowned. "Are you quitting?"

He scowled at me. "Yes."

"Why?"

His shoulders lifted, then dropped as he expelled a violent breath.

"It should be obvious."

"Well, it's not."

"You won't marry me. I… I can't stay here anymore. It hurts too much."

"So, you're going to abandon your son?"

As my voice grew in volume, he grabbed my arm and ushered me into my office. He motioned to a chair as he closed the door.

"I'm not abandoning anyone. However, I am protecting myself. I want Remi to live with me on the weekends. I'll come pick him up after supper on Fridays. Then he can go home with you after church on Sundays. Or I'll bring him home Sunday afternoon. Whatever makes you happy."

I crossed my arms over my chest. None of what he said made me happy. Instead, it cut open old wounds and created a few new ones.

"You want to take him from me?"

He sighed and rolled his eyes.

"No. What I want is to marry you and be a real bona fide family. But you refuse me. So, I'm asking for a compromise. One that lets me be a father to my son. It gives you what you want, and it gives me a chance to move on, but still be Remi's father."

None of it was what I wanted. I wanted… I didn't know what I wanted.

Yes, I did. I wanted a guarantee that Preston wouldn't leave me. That he wouldn't start drinking again.

"Hetty, all you have to do is say that you'll marry me. I'll stay here. Give up my plans to open the stables."

What was he talking about? What stables?

"I'm ready for marriage."

"I'm not." The words flew out of my mouth before I could stop them.

The hurt in his eyes matched the pain I felt when he abandoned me. I knew that pain. Now I was the one inflicting it. A whisper of guilt nudged my heart, but I ignored it.

Preston's head hung low as he slowly stood. "I'll be back in a few weeks. We can discuss Remi more then."

Then he walked out the door, taking my heart with him.

I propped my arms on Papa's smooth desk. Then I lowered my head and rested it on my arms. Rivers of tears ran down my face and dripped onto the desktop as my soul cried out.

After several minutes, the numbness replaced the pain. I straightened and blotted the puddle of tears off the desk. Then I tallied the ledgers as if it was a normal day on the ranch and not the day I pushed Preston away.

At supper, I said little. I glanced at Preston's empty chair. In time, it would hurt less. At least that was the lie I told myself.

"Papa?" Remi asked.

My eyes burned. "He took a trip with Grandpa Will and Grandma Hannah."

Remi's lower lip quivered. "Play Papa."

Mama smoothed out his hair. "He'll be back in a few weeks."

Remi slid his plate away. "Brandy potty."

I sighed and pushed back from the table. Then I opened the back door while Remi and Brandy stood in the yard. Brandy did her business before the two came back inside.

Remi took her to his room and curled up on the bed. Brandy whined before she licked his hand. Tears trailed down my cheeks as I walked away from the scene.

When I joined Mama in the parlor, I stared at the fire while I sipped some coffee.

"You did this to yourself, Hetty Adelaide."

Tension seeped into my shoulders. Mama never used my middle name. Not unless I was in trouble.

"Why are you being so stubborn? The man has changed. Dramatically. He loves you. He wants to be with you. You could have your happily ever after."

I snorted. "It might not be happily ever after. He could start drinking again."

Mama scowled. "And you could reject him enough times that he gives up on you."

I launched to my feet. Then I rushed from the house and stomped to the barn. How was it my fault? I was the injured party. He left me behind.

As I walked toward White Lightning's stall, I glanced at Ranger's empty one. Empty like my heart.

Anger simmered. Preston made his choice. If he didn't want to wait for me, then so be it.

Even as my thoughts tried to blame him for my current pain, deep down I knew it was a self-inflicted wound. It didn't matter. He was gone. I would let him go. I didn't need Preston Colter.

CHAPTER 26

PRESTON

I was far from home. So very far from home. As dusk settled over Colter Ranch, I felt myself fading away like the light. I was not where I belonged. No, I belonged at Clark Ranch. Not just at the ranch, but also in the ranch house. I belonged by Hetty's side. Instead, she left me to play the lone hand.

As I carried the lantern to Uncle Adam's house, I shoved away the thoughts. Hetty didn't want me. I would not let that destroy me. I had a plan for my life. So, I would move on. Let her be lonely and bitter if that was the path she chose. It didn't have to be mine.

"Evening," Aunt Julia greeted me when I opened the door. "You eat?"

"Yeah. Had supper with the family."

"That's good. I'm sure your parents appreciate you being home."

Home. Colter Ranch wasn't that. Not anymore. It was where I grew up but wasn't my home.

"Let me finish helping Julia with the dishes. Then we can talk," Uncle Adam said.

After I sat at the table, I sipped my coffee and watched my aunt and uncle with fresh eyes. Even though I had studied them while they worked with the horses, I missed how seamlessly they interacted with each other.

As I sat there, it occurred to me how deeply they loved each other. Adam touched her hand as he took a dish from her to dry it. She smiled at him. A look. A touch. They said a lot with only a few words.

"How long have you been married?" The question popped out of my mouth.

Julia glanced over her shoulder and smiled. "Forever."

Adam laughed.

"You don't know, do you?" he teased.

Her cheeks flushed. "Not long enough?"

He shook his head as he set the last dish aside. Then he pulled her close. "If you come up with the right answer, you'll win a kiss."

"Twenty-eight years on Saturday." She grinned.

I smiled as I averted my gaze while my uncle kissed his wife.

When they sat down, the smile still shone in his eyes, and Julia's cheeks remained pink. Adam's gaze tore away from her as he sipped his coffee.

"Speaking of Saturday," Adam said, turning his attention toward me. "I'll join you up in Ash Fork on Monday. We have plans for our anniversary."

"Completely understand."

"Besides, it'll let us transport the horses in two groups. You can take some up on Friday. I'll bring the rest on Monday."

"You think twelve is enough to start?" Julia asked. "Maybe we should send more."

Adam squeezed her hand. "I don't want to deplete our

stock here. With Preston being in Ash Fork along the Atlantic & Pacific railroad, it'll be easier to have fresh stock delivered there."

She smiled. "I can't believe this is really happening."

"Neither can I," I said.

"We've talked about expanding for years. I'm glad you want to take this on."

"I'm grateful you're trusting me with part of your business." I wish Hetty had that much faith in me. If she did… It was useless dwelling on it.

"Of course," Adam said. "You've always been a large part of what we do at Larson Stables. It makes sense to partner with you on it."

Some people, perhaps even my brothers, would insist on calling the Ash Fork branch of the business Colter Stables. If James had been back from his Chicago trip, he would have vehemently argued for it.

Putting Papa's name on another business didn't matter to me. Sure, it was my name, too. But Uncle Adam and Aunt Julia built the business from almost nothing. He brought the original stud with him from Texas. He and Julia put in years of blood and sweat. It was their business and ought to carry their name.

Especially since he had no sons to carry the name. The thought brought a pang of homesickness for my own son. He might not share my name. He may never share it. But he shared my blood. I would build the business in Ash Fork. Then I could be as much of a father to him as Hetty would allow.

"You miss him, don't you?" Julia asked.

I nodded, wondering how she read my thoughts.

She sighed. "It was hard when two of my girls married and left the ranch. Caty is in town, but Penny moved away with her husband. Only Dory is still home, though she'll find someone soon. She's helping Caty this week."

Adam squeezed my shoulder. "You're doing the right thing. Sticking close to him and building a life for yourself up there."

"Thanks." I just wished it didn't feel so terrible.

We spent the next hour planning which horses to move and which would stay.

"Too bad you couldn't take Thomas's leatherwork with you," Adam said.

"No need for it," I said. "My friend Brian owns a saddlery. And Rich owns the livery. Both are fine craftsmen."

Aunt Julia leaned back. "You've really put down roots up there, haven't you?"

I told them how my posse helped each other through rough times.

"Five, huh?" Julia smiled.

My eyebrow raised.

"Silly, five Colter brothers. Five men in your posse. You are a blessed man, Preston Colter."

———

Friday morning, I rode Ranger in the lead as Adam and Julia rode flank, pushing the six horses toward my position. It was easier to drive them that way than dealing with so many leads. They were all broke, so they followed our direction well.

After we loaded them and Ranger onto the train, I hugged Aunt Julia and Uncle Adam goodbye.

"I'll see you in a few days," Adam said.

"I'll be praying for you," Julia said. "Not just for the business."

Then I boarded the train and headed home.

Home. Almost. Not the home of my heart. Perhaps in time, Rich's house would feel like mine, too.

The woman on the train next to me fidgeted with her reticule. She seemed rather nervous, and I was tired of thinking about my relationship woes, so I struck up a conversation with her.

"First time on the train?" I asked.

"No. I… I'm moving to Ash Fork."

"Oh? That's where I'm headed, too. Starting up Larson Stables."

"Larson Stables? Is it moving?"

"You've heard of them?"

"Of course. Anyone who knows anything about horse-flesh knows about Larson Stables."

I smiled, twice as glad that I didn't insist on naming it after me. Adam's reputation was known far and wide.

"Larson is my uncle, so I'm opening a branch up in Ash Fork."

She nodded and went back to fidgeting with her reticule.

"You have family up there?" I asked.

"In a way. My husband, Thomas, works for the railroad. He's the station manager."

"Thomas Erwin?" I couldn't believe it. Thomas never mentioned he had a wife.

"We've been estranged for a while."

"I know him. He's a close friend of mine."

She relaxed against the seat back. "So, you can tell me if he's truly done drinking, then?"

"Yes, ma'am. I've known him since April and have not seen him drink a drop."

I wondered how much Thomas told her about our posse.

"If you aren't, this will sound weird." She sighed. "Are you one of his posse?"

I laughed. "Yes."

"Does it help?"

"Meeting together?"

She nodded.

"It does. We've formed a deep friendship. We help each other. In fact, they'll be waiting to help me with the horses when we arrive."

The conversation waned until we neared Ash Fork.

"My name is Sybil, by the way."

"Name's Preston. Preston Colter."

When the train stopped, I helped Sybil down. Then I escorted her toward the stock cars since that's where the posse was going to meet me.

The reunion between Thomas and Sybil seemed awkward. The love in his eyes was clear, while the fear in hers kept him from greeting her like I'm sure he wanted to. He apologized to me for not being able to help with the horses. Then he escorted her away.

"Did you know he was married?" I asked Rich.

"He mentioned it once before you joined the posse. Then the day we helped find Remi, he told us she was moving here."

"He didn't know what train she'd be on?" I asked.

"She was supposed to come on Monday last week," Brian said. "Don't worry, we'll get the dirt from him on Wednesday."

I laughed. "You're worse than the old biddies at the mercantile."

"Let's get your horses to their new home," Rich said as he slapped me on the back.

We corralled the horses in less than an hour. Adam provided the money for a tract of land north of town. Over the coming weeks, Rich, Clyde, and Brian were going to help me build a barn and corral. I'd continue living with Rich until one or the other of us settled down.

It wouldn't be me. Not unless Hetty miraculously decided she would marry me. Since that wasn't gonna happen, my money was on Rich, falling in love first.

CHAPTER 27

November 12, 1893

HETTY

Remi and I settled into a routine with Preston. On Friday afternoons, Preston picked up Remi for the weekend. Then on Sunday, I brought him home with me after church. A few times, Preston brought him home later in the afternoon.

It was painful every week. Even though I got used to it, I hated it.

When Remi was with his father, I missed him. The weekends seemed long and empty without my son. I even missed the chaos of trying to get him ready for church.

Brandy jumped into my bed on Sunday morning, and she licked my face.

"Alright. I'm up."

I threw back the covers and slipped my bare feet into my boots as I donned my coat over my nightgown. After opening the back door, I entered the yard. Brandy took care of business. Then she wiggled her little butt and started chasing something. Only she knew what it was.

"Come on, spunky girl. I need some coffee."

When she barked her playful bark, I smiled. She seemed to know it was Sunday and that she'd see her Remi soon.

After another minute, she bounded into the house. She'd grown a lot since Remi's birthday. She stood knee high and all her fluffy puppy fur settled into a smoother coat. Once inside, she shook and took up the vigil at the front window.

Rita handed me a mug of coffee. Before I set it on the table, I took a big gulp. Then I hurried back to my room. I stared at my three dresses with a frown. Normally, I wore one to church on Sunday. That day, I opted for my britches. I had no one to impress, anyway.

Mama and I limited our conversation at breakfast. Since Preston left, at least once a week Mama mentioned something about him. How she missed seeing him at supper. If he lived at the ranch, he could spend more time with his son. I knew her motives. She hoped if he was around all the time that he'd wear me down and I would finally marry him.

As I walked to the barn to saddle White Lightning, I shook my head. The longer I went without Preston around, the less likely I would ever marry him. Of course, I missed him. He still owned my heart. But I couldn't get past my fears.

Rio asked a cowboy to ready the carriage, so once I had my horse saddled, I rode to town. My morning ride as catawampus as my heart.

When I dismounted outside of church, I noticed Preston walking down the street from Rich's house. He knocked on a door. A beautiful blond woman in a stylish pink dress stepped from the house. She smiled as he offered his arm.

My heart lodged in my throat as I ducked down behind White Lightning. It was silly. He knew my horse and could still see my legs.

As I straightened, I looked down at my britches and blue shirt. Then I glanced at the woman's gorgeous dress. Embar-rassed, I hurried into the church.

"Morning, Hetty," Iris greeted me.

"Morning."

As the doors opened behind me, I glanced back. Preston, Remi, and the lady in pink entered.

"Mama!" Remi squealed and ran toward me.

The lady in pink frowned as she watched Remi launch himself into my arms. I hugged my little boy close while I glared at the lady in pink.

Preston stepped to the side and motioned for her to slide into the pew where he usually sat. My heart ached. He had moved on from me. I hadn't expected it to happen so quickly. He had only left two months ago.

Mama entered the building, followed by a stream of parishioners. I stood next to our usual pew.

"Do you want to sit with me or Papa?" I asked Remi.

He looked at Preston. Then me. "Papa."

I set him down. "Go."

He ran to Preston, who scooped him up into his lap. Preston's smile melted my heart. He loved our son so much.

A tear slipped from my eye. I wiped it away as I sat down and faced forward.

"Who is with Preston?" Mama asked me.

Like I would know. Thankfully, the music started, cutting off a response I didn't want to give.

When Clyde stood, he asked us to turn to the passage where Peter asked how many times he ought to forgive his brother.

"Not seven times, but seventy-seven times."

I crossed my arms over my chest.

"Jesus wasn't telling Peter to forgive a literal number of times. No, he meant we are to forgive as many times and as often as it takes. If someone wrongs me and I remember it and stew over it again, even though I already forgave him, I need to forgive him again."

When he said the last words, he looked directly at me. I narrowed my eyes. Once he looked away, I stood and walked out of the church. I knew what Clyde was telling me. I needed to forgive Preston again.

Not that simple. I forgave Preston. I just didn't trust the changes he made were permanent. There was a difference.

But was there really?

I cut him out because I didn't want to get hurt again. Yet, I was miserable. I thought about him all the time. In my imagination, I argued with him. What if he drank again? Would I keep Remi from him?

As I paced back and forth in front of the church stairs, my stomach tightened. I should let it go. Take a leap of faith.

The church doors opened as people filed out. The lady in pink clutched Preston's arm. When he saw me, he nodded. Then he walked toward me.

"Let me take Sybil home. Then I'll gather Remi's things and you can take him home."

The lady in pink's name was Sybil. I glared at her.

"Is that alright?" he asked.

I nodded and watched him walk Sybil back to her house. At least he had the decency not to kiss her while I was watching.

A few minutes later, he returned with Remi's things. I tossed them on the floor of the carriage.

"Thanks."

When he said goodbye to Remi, he gave me a strange

look. Then he stepped closer. I frowned.

"How are you doing, Hetty?"

"Fine." I supposed I should try to be friendly. "How is your new business?"

"Good. The Aztec Land & Cattle Company contracted Larson Stables for a steady supply of horses."

"That's the outfit with a million acres east of here, right?" I asked numbly.

"Yup."

His blue eyes locked on mine. After he opened and closed his mouth several times, he finally stepped back. "I'll see you on Friday."

Once I made sure Remi sat in the carriage with Mama, I mounted White Lightning and rode home. I was happy for him with his business. Really.

It was Sybil I had a problem with. I wondered where she came from and how long he had known her. Did he wait a week or a month after he left to start seeing her?

I didn't know why I was so upset. I was the one that declined his proposal. More than once. I shouldn't hold it against him as he moved on. He deserved a chance at happiness.

The rest of the afternoon, I sulked around the house while Remi played with Brandy. She nearly licked his face off when he came home. That dog loved him so much. Maybe I would suggest to Preston he should take them both next week. Give me a break from caring for the dog, and it would let her stay with Remi.

I wished Papa was there. He'd know what I should do about Preston.

CHAPTER 28

PRESTON

Seeing Hetty at the church was odd. We spoke about things on a surface level, both of us trying not to engage our hearts. It nearly crushed me how impersonal we became in such a short amount of time. If it wasn't for my posse, I wasn't sure I'd make it through the loss of her without drinking.

"What's on your mind?" Rich asked as he sat down for supper.

I appreciated him giving me a room in his house, and for putting up with a two-year-old on weekends.

"Hetty."

Rich shook his head as he took a bite of his food. "I don't know why the two of you are making yourselves so miserable."

I snorted. "She won't marry me."

"So? Does that mean you should stop pursuing her?"

"It hurts too much."

"Ha. From where I sit, it looks just as painful not pursuing her."

I swallowed a bite of food. He was right. I was miserable

either way. At least Larson Stables consumed a lot of my time.

"Oh, this came for you," he said as he slid a letter across the table.

When I picked up the envelope, I immediately recognized Deacon's neat script. His writing was as meticulous as everything else about him.

"You mind if I read it now?"

"Go ahead."

I sliced the envelope open and unfolded the paper. Then I read it silently.

He asked how Remi was. And about Larson Stables. Then he reminded me he proposed to Lilian Harper.

"I would like you to stand for me at our wedding on Christmas Day." I read the words.

Then I coughed as I lowered the paper to the table and stared at it.

"What is it?" Rich asked.

"Deacon wants me to stand for him at his wedding."

"That's good, right?"

I nodded as I continued to read Deacon's words. "I'm sure you assumed I would ask Grady. Even though we're close friends, he's not my blood brother. You are. I don't know when we drifted apart."

That was easy. It was when Grady moved to the ranch.

"We should be close like we used to be. So, please tell me you'll do it. Stand for me as my brother and my friend."

When he moved on to other news, I set the letter aside to read it later.

"What put that frown on your face?"

I sighed. Sometimes Rich's invasiveness bothered me. I knew he cared about my best interests when he asked.

"Nothing."

"Well, if you want to talk…"

After supper, I washed dishes, and Rich dried them. Then I took the letter to my room and reread it.

Deacon asked me to stand for him. I had a hard time believing Grady accepted it. I scanned the letter again. No, he said Grady would stand for him as well, but I would hold the place of honor.

Me.

I shook my head in disbelief. Then I wrote my reply. Of course, I would stand for him.

———

Thanksgiving Day was bittersweet. For the first time in years, I faced the day dry and clear-headed. That brought me joy. The sadness came with missing everyone that was dear to me. My parents. My brothers and their families. Vi. Hetty. Remi.

As I opened the door to the Caldwell's house, I greeted them. Most of the posse already sat around the table. Thomas and his wife, Sybil. Brian. Clyde and Iris.

Rich and I took the remaining open seats before Clyde offered a prayer. When he finished, I caught a flush on Sybil's cheek as Thomas released her hand. It was good to see the two of them slowly repairing their relationship.

A few weeks ago, he asked me to escort her to church while he traveled to Prescott for a meeting with several managers at the railroad's headquarters. Sybil had confided in me she worried about him and hoped he'd stay out of trouble. He did, and that alone went a long way towards repairing things between them.

When I learned they had been living apart for nearly two years, it made me sad. It took her that long to be ready to trust him again. I'd only given Hetty a few months.

Perhaps my expectations had been unrealistic. Instead of pressuring her into a long-term relationship, I should concentrate on the business and staying sober.

At a break in the conversation, I said, "My family's tradition is sharing something we are thankful for. So, I am thankful for my posse and my son. Also, for my new life that started the morning after I should have died."

Everyone nodded their heads. When Sybil quirked her eyebrow, I took a minute to explain what had happened the night of the fire.

"And I'm grateful to the Caldwells for taking me in," I finished.

"I'm thankful Sybil is here in Ash Fork," Thomas said as he gazed upon his wife fondly. "And that she's willing to give me another chance."

Pink colored her cheeks as he squeezed her hand.

"Your turn," he whispered.

"I… Um… I'm thankful for the posse and how you've helped Thomas change."

"That change came from God and Thomas being willing," Clyde said.

Sybil nodded before she looked down at her plate. She clearly held some reservations about her husband.

"I'm thankful for all of you," Rich said. "My life would be empty without friends like you."

A smile curved my lips as I agreed. Our friendship meant the world to me, too.

"I'm thankful for a letter from my mama," Brian said.

"When did that arrive?" Clyde asked.

"Yesterday afternoon. Papa passed a few years ago. She wants to see me and invited me for a visit."

"That's wonderful news," I said as I squeezed his shoulder.

"Yeah. It sounded like she's been sharing my letters with my sisters, too."

"You think you'll go?" Rich asked.

"Maybe early next year. I'll see how the next few letters go. With Papa gone, it makes it easier. Maybe I can learn who Mama is without him."

He cleared his throat. "Iris, how about you? What are you thankful for?"

She sighed and set her silverware down. "I'm thankful to be part of this community. And to meet and pray for such wonderful people, like all of you. You bring me joy."

I shifted in my chair as the feelings of failure and worthlessness tried to push forward. The thought that I would bring joy to someone like Iris left me speechless.

"I meant it," she said. She looked at each of us. "Each of you brings me joy. Even though I'm not part of your meetings, I've seen the change in each of you as I welcome you into my home. I see how you help each other. That doesn't happen by accident. That happens because you've allowed God to work in your hearts and change you from the inside out. I'm blessed to witness it."

"And we're blessed to eat your good cooking," Brian said with a grin.

The silence stretched for a few minutes. Then Clyde finally spoke.

"I am thankful and humbled to be Iris's husband. We had several rough years. They were dark, and she should have left me, but she prayed for me instead."

He made eye contact with each of us. "There is nothing as powerful as a praying woman. My life is proof of it. I know I don't talk about the distant past much. But you know my story. It mirrors yours. Thomas, Sybil, ours is eerily similar to yours.”

“So, I am thankful for the prayers of my wife. And that God put a passion for His Word in my heart. And that He uses me to come alongside the likes of you all.”

“Thank you, Preston, for suggesting this,” Iris said. “It’s good to reflect on how far we’ve come.”

She reached across Brian to pat my arm.

“Now, who’s ready for dessert?”

We all laughed and helped clear the dishes while she and Sybil dished up the pie.

I may not have spent the day with my birth family, but it brought me joy to spend the day with my spiritual family.

After we left the Caldwells, Rich and I headed out to the Larson Stables’ property to care for the horses. As I brushed down a mare, she pranced, and her ears flicked.

“What is it?” I whispered to her.

She snorted and backed away. Then she grew antsy. I carefully backed out of the stall.

“Rich?”

“Yeah?”

“I’m gonna ride the perimeter. Something’s bothering Macy.”

“Want me to come?”

I stood in front of the stall he occupied with a two-year-old.

“Naw. I’m probably just being paranoid.”

“Alright. Fire off a shot if you run into anything.”

Ranger was still saddled from our ride out to the property, so I mounted up and we rode the fence line. When I reached the farthest section, a dust cloud swirled up from the ground.

The sting of a bullet slicing my arm came before my mind registered the sound. Gunshots erupted around me, and I kicked Ranger to a gallop away from there.

As a bullet pierced my back, I stiffened. Then the pain knocked me off Ranger. When my body hit the ground, my eyes blurred. Blackness swallowed me.

CHAPTER 29

HETTY

As we sat down for Thanksgiving dinner, Remi said, "Miss Papa."

Mama frowned. Not at him, but at me.

"I know, I know. I should have invited him."

I sighed heavily.

"We'll make the best of the day since I didn't."

"You could ride into town with Remi and let him spend time with him, anyway."

Mama's words chafed me. We'd had a similar discussion for a week. If it wasn't about Thanksgiving, then it was about me being stubborn.

As I stuffed a bite of mashed potatoes in my mouth, I stopped myself from glaring at my mother. I knew she meant well.

"We'll see."

He was probably spending the day with that Sybil lady, anyway.

When we finished the meal, Mama and I washed the dishes so Rita could spend the afternoon with Rio. Mav took Remi and Brandy over to the bunkhouse to give Mama and me a brief break.

"Hetty."

I closed my eyes at the tone in Mama's voice. Then I pasted on a smile while I waited for the chiding to begin.

"Have you ever wondered why you don't have any brothers or sisters?"

That question smacked me as hard as a stick of dynamite blasting through a collapsed mine shaft.

"Your father and I weren't as happy as what you remember. Before you were born, things were… Difficult. Unhappy."

"What do you mean?"

"I… I don't want to color the memories you have of your father."

As I dried a plate, I waited for her to continue.

"One reason Matt refused John Bartholomew's offer was because he remembers how much it hurt me when he…"

Mama's voice faded.

"Your father. Before he knew Jesus, he was a terrible husband. He spent many nights at a rum mill with other women. He'd come home the next morning reeking of liquor."

"Papa drank?"

"Yes, back in Texas he drank, and he was unfaithful."

Mama gripped the edge of the sink for several seconds. "He was very unkind when he drank."

My stomach tightened as I filled in the holes of her story. He beat her. Papa. My loving, saintly father beat the woman he loved more than life. I just couldn't picture it.

Mama's green eyes rimmed with red as she looked into mine. "Hetty, if God can change a man like your father into all the wonderful things you remember about him, don't you think He can change Preston?"

A frown settled over my face as my breathing shallowed. My heart pounded in my chest as my mind tried to comprehend.

Mama dried her hands on a towel. Then she placed them on my cheeks. "Sweet girl, you were born into a troubled marriage to an angry, drunk man who changed. Once you were born, something unlocked in his heart. A child, you triggered a permanent change in him."

Her hands dropped to her side.

"Don't you think God can work the same miracle in your son's father's heart?"

No words came. My head hurt thinking about what she said. Papa changed because of me. Everything I thought I knew about him… All that came after I was born.

I cleared my throat. "Why don't I have siblings?"

"I don't really know. Our relationship changed for the better after your arrival. But I never conceived again. Not sure why. It didn't matter, though. Matt became a new man. My soulmate. My forever love."

"You have been the greatest joy of our lives. Your birth has always been a tangible reminder of when our marriage truly began. Did you know we celebrated our anniversary the day after your birthday and not the day we actually married?"

I shook my head.

"That was the most important change in Matt. The night after you were born, he promised me he would become a different man. Never again to touch a bottle. Never again to be with another woman. It was the three of us."

Mama's shoulders dropped as she sighed. "I want that kind of love for you. Preston is the man your heart chose long ago. He loves his son, and he loves you even more. It's been seven months. How much longer are you going to make him pay for hurting you?"

"I'm not making him pay."

"Oh, but you are. You pretend that you're protecting your heart. You aren't. Instead, you're exacting revenge on him by withholding the one thing he desires more than anything—a life with you."

"And you're making the both of you miserable. You're robbing Remi of the family he deserves. For what reason?"

She cleared her throat.

"Now, go. Take your son to his father. Spend the rest of the afternoon with him."

When she finished speaking, she turned me toward the door and nudged me.

I walked out the front door, shocked and numb. Mav had the carriage waiting. Clearly, Mama conspired with him. Remi sat there with Brandy laying at his feet.

"See Papa?"

His blue eyes looked so hopeful.

"Yes. We'll go see your papa."

I climbed onto the seat next to him. Then I started the carriage forward as Mama's words echoed in my mind. Perhaps she was right. The deeper motive of my heart may have been to make Preston pay for abandoning me and Remi.

Ugh.

How could I continue to refuse him if my father was a shining example that a man could change so completely, so permanently?

Lord, forgive me for holding on to bitterness toward Preston and for not trusting the changes You've been making in his heart. He is a completely different person.

A tear of regret slipped from my eye, and I wiped it away. I needed to tell him how I felt. I must ask Preston for his forgiveness. My heart wanted him. I was ready at last.

When I pulled the carriage up next to Rich's house, I thought it seemed eerily quiet. I knocked on the door several times. Since no one answered, I opened it.

Empty.

My heart squeezed tight.

"Come on, Remi, let's see if he's at the Caldwell's. Bring Brandy."

"Come Brandy."

Her back end bounced as we walked the short distance to their home. When I knocked on their door, Clyde smiled as he opened it.

"Hetty, Remi, what brings you by?"

"Have you seen Preston? We went by Rich's house, but no one was home. We thought it might be nice to visit for a few hours."

Iris greeted us as we entered their home.

"We ate an early meal and finished before one," she said.

"He and Rich left hours ago to take care of the horses," Thomas said as we stepped into the parlor.

I held back a frown when I saw Sybil was there. She seemed unconcerned that no one had seen Preston.

When Thomas took a seat next to her and held her hand, my stomach clenched. I glanced at her hand. A wedding band.

Wait.

"Have you met my wife?" Thomas asked. Then he introduced me to Sybil.

I ignored the question, pressing against the tip of my tongue. Instead, I asked, "So, Preston and Rich have been gone since one?"

"That's right," Brian said. "They ought to be back by now."

Fear constricted my throat.

"Iris, can you watch Remi? Clyde, do you think Rich would mind if I borrowed a horse?"

"We'll come with you," Brian said as he and Thomas rose to their feet.

Clyde followed us to the livery, where we saddled up horses before we rode out to Larson Stables.

When we arrived, there was no sign of anyone at the stables. My gut screamed something was very wrong.

Then I saw them a short distance away. Blood covered Rich's arms and splotched his undershirt as he leaned over a man on the ground.

"Preston!" His name wrenched free from my throat as I ran toward them.

My breathing sounded loud in my ears. My heart drowned out other noises. I sank to my knees next to his lifeless body. My eyes burned.

I was too late.

CHAPTER 30

HETTY

"Help her." Clyde's voice sounded far off.

"Hetty." Thomas's soothing voice registered in my ears as he hefted me from the ground.

Someone screamed. Loud wails filled the air. Coming from my throat.

"He's not dead."

"Barely alive," Brian muttered. He lifted Preston's feet as Rich and Clyde carried him to a wagon.

How long had I stood there?

"They shot him," Rich said.

I climbed into the bed of the wagon next to Preston's still body.

"In the back. I barely got the bleeding stopped when you showed up."

"Got to get him to the doctor."

"Hannah." Her name dropped from my lips. "We have to wire Hannah."

"We'll wire his family after we know more," Clyde said as Brian drove the wagon back to town.

"She knows medicine. She'll want to help," I said.

Thomas patted my arm. "Let's see what the doctor says first. No need to scare his mama with partial news."

I clasped Preston's hand in mine. It was cold. Pale. Like his face. No color.

He was in terrible shape. I'd seen enough gunshot wounds to know this wasn't good.

"The bullet?" I asked.

"As far as I know, still in him."

A sob escaped from my mouth. *Please Lord. Please.*

"I'm so sorry," I whispered. "So sorry."

As Clyde, Rich, and Brian carried him into the doctor's office, I watched numbly.

Then Clyde led me to the waiting room. I sat as my heart died in my chest. I waited too long. If only I had believed in him sooner and accepted the change in him. He would have stayed at the ranch. We'd be home around the fire watching our son play with his dog.

Instead, he laid in the next room as the life faded from his body. He was leaving me forever. The sobs shook my body. Comforting arms encircled me.

"Shh," Iris whispered. "He's not gone yet. We can still pray."

My heart had no words to offer in prayer. I listened as she whispered words to the Miracle Worker. Requests for healing. Pleading for his life. My soul cried the words along with her.

Please.

In time, the sobs softened. Then I rested my head on her shoulder and closed my eyes.

When a sound came from down the hall, I shot to my feet. I clutched my hands in front of me as if they could protect the last bit of life in my heart.

"How is he?" I pleaded for an answer.

"He's sleeping."

The energy seeped from my legs, and they felt mushy beneath me. Clyde held me upright.

"We got the bullet out. But he's lost a lot of blood. Time will tell."

Time will tell?! No. I needed to hear better news. That he'd be alright. I wanted the promises. I wanted to know. Know. Not a guess. No maybes.

"Come, let's get you home. You need some rest."

My legs moved with Clyde's as he held me up. Iris walked to my other side as they led me to their home to a bed.

As soon as I laid down, sleep overtook me.

———

When I woke up the next morning, I enjoyed a few seconds of peace before the memories of Preston's pale face invaded. I shot upright in the unfamiliar room before I jerked the door open.

"Where is he?"

"Remi is with Thomas and Sybil. It would be better if he didn't see you in this state," Iris said.

My son. Some mother I was. I completely forgot I brought him to town yesterday.

"Preston?"

Clyde cleared his throat. "Made it through the night."

As I collapsed into a chair at their table, Iris set a coffee in front of me.

"Brian rode out this morning to your ranch to let your mama know you are alright. He promised to bring back a change of clothes for you and Remi," Clyde said.

"You're welcome to stay with us as long as you'd like,"

Iris said.

"And we can bring Remi over whenever you want. Just say the word."

After I propped my arms on the table, I rested my head in my hands. Preston. What had I done? What life did I miss because of my stubbornness?

"Thomas promised to wire the Colters this morning after getting an update from the doctor," Clyde said.

"I'm sure they will come if they can," Iris said. "We have space for them if they do."

My thoughts continued to accuse me harshly throughout the morning and on into the next day. Several days. I didn't know. Time seemed to pass by incredibly slowly. I wasn't aware of the day of the week. Only what happened to Preston.

Several days passed. They finally let me see him once they moved him to his home. He should be at my home. By my side.

His mother and father came. They stayed with him, never leaving his bedside. I sat on the other side, clutching his hand, willing him to take my strength for his own.

At some point, Mama took Remi and Brandy home. Rio brought White Lightning and boarded him at the livery.

One afternoon, Will suggested a ride out to the stables. "Someone needs to care for the horses. Might be good to get some fresh air."

So, I saddled my horse. He saddled one from the livery. Then the two of us rode out.

"You can't blame yourself for this," he said. "No one besides the rustlers is responsible. Preston was in the wrong place at the wrong time."

The circumstances didn't matter to my heart. Regret tried to drown me. I wanted to let it.

Instead, I went through the soothing motions of taking care of Preston's horses. Doing his job to keep his business running while he fought for his life. I knew that was Will's plan, too. We'd make sure his business survived.

When we returned to the house that afternoon, Hannah's face shrouded in fear.

"He's got a fever. I've mixed up a poultice to draw out the infection."

As I sat next to him, I watched as she placed the healing medicine over the festering wound on his back. He moaned and flinched. After she finished, she left his back facing up with his face turned to the side.

When they left the room, I pushed his overgrown hair out of his face.

"Please, Preston. I'm so sorry I pushed you away. Please come back to me. I love you. I want to be your wife."

A sob wrangled free from my throat.

"I want you to be my husband."

Sweat beaded on his forehead. I blotted it dry with a cloth. Over and over as I waited for him to return to me.

CHAPTER 31

PRESTON

My skin felt icy, like I stood outside in the middle of a snowstorm with no coat and no fire to warm me. I wanted to open my eyes, but the lids felt too heavy. Wouldn't budge.

Then the heat. Fire like I stood inside of a fireplace. Heat singed my skin. Burning. Pain.

Silence. Quiet.

Then a soft hand touched my face. Mama?

Where was I?

"Mama?"

"I'm here, son."

Oh good. She'd fix up whatever was wrong with me. I relaxed against the bed.

Words of prayer. Papa's deep voice rang in my ears.

I remembered sitting in the saddle with him. His big hand held me steady. Laughter rang around me. I giggled. Horsey fun.

Remi pressed up next to me in my saddle. My hand seemed so big. I was a father. I had a son.

His mother. Where was she?

Blond hair. Green eyes. That sassy smile. I loved that smile. She won. I knew she would.

It was hot again. Stifling. Sweat soaked my shirt. It must be summer. I should find some shade.

Hetty touched my face, and her calloused hands felt tender.

"I love you."

I know.

"I want to marry you."

A sob.

Don't cry, Hetty. I want to marry you, too. There's only one woman for me. It is you.

"I want you to be my husband."

Mmmm. I could see it. Me at Clark Ranch. Waking up to her smiling face. It was how things ought to be.

"Hetty?"

My lips felt sticky. My throat was dry. I tried to move, but my arms weighed too much.

"Hetty?"

"Preston?"

Fear? Joy? I couldn't place the emotion in her voice.

My eyelids crept open. I blinked.

"Thank you, God!"

Her green eyes looked even greener than normal, with the red rings around them. Dark circles rested under them.

"What?"

Speaking required too much energy.

"Here, let us help you up."

"Mama?"

"Your parents are here."

Hetty's beautiful face moved away too soon, replaced by Mama's comforting one.

Once I sat up, the pain in my back knocked the wind

from me.

"Here, sip this," Mama said.

After I choked down the bitter willow bark tea, she plied me with some broth. Then I grew sleepy again.

I faded in and out often, with no obvious sense of time passing.

Then, one day, I felt stronger. Stayed awake longer.

"What happened?" I asked Papa.

"Some rustlers shot you. Rich didn't think they stole any of the horses. Hetty reviewed your records, and all the horses were accounted for."

I looked around the room. "Where is she?"

"Out taking care of the horses."

"I should be there."

Mama placed a hand on my shoulder. "You should be here. Resting."

I frowned.

"Do you want to see Remi?"

"Absolutely."

"I'll go get him," Papa said.

A while later, Papa brought Remi into the room.

"Papa?" he whispered.

I held my arms open wide. My papa set him on the bed next to me.

"Remember, be gentle."

Remi nodded. "Yes, Gampa."

My little boy seemed like he'd grown a few more inches since I last saw him. His round eyes warmed my heart.

"Lean up against me."

He rested his head on my belly. Then he lightly placed his arm around my waist. I settled my arm around him.

"Love you."

My eyes burned at his declaration. I cleared my throat.

"Love you too, Remi."

Exhaustion tugged at me, so I fell asleep with him snuggled against me.

———

HETTY

Two weeks had passed since the rustlers shot Preston. His strength grew each day. Hannah thought he'd be ready for solid food soon. She mentioned she and Will would return home in a few days. Deacon's wedding was two weeks away. We all hoped Preston would be well enough to travel to Colter Ranch for it.

When I returned from Larson Stables, I straightened my back and pushed the door of his room open. My heart fluttered at the sight of Remi tucked under Preston's arm, both resting quietly. I eased into the chair next to him.

"Come here," he whispered as one eye peeked open.

He patted the bed next to him.

"I don't want to hurt you."

He smiled. "You won't."

I gently, slowly reclined on the bed next to him. Then I rested my arm on his chest. His warm arm came around my back.

"Did you talk to me while I was sleeping?" he asked.

"Yes."

His hand rubbed my arm. "What did you say?"

My cheeks warmed at the memory of my words. I wasn't sure if it was the right time.

"Please, tell me."

I sighed.

"I said a lot of things."

As I sat up, I made sure not to bump into him. Then I gazed into his eyes.

"I'm sorry, Preston. I'm sorry I didn't trust you."

He brought his hand up to cup my face in it. Then his thumb rubbed across my cheek. I saw his deep love for me in those ridiculously handsome blue eyes.

"I love you," I whispered. "If you... If you still want me..."

The words clogged my throat, and I looked away.

"I do."

My gaze found his again.

"I want you to be my husband."

My fingers pushed his dark hair back from his face. Red rimmed his eyes as his throat worked. I leaned forward, careful to keep my weight on my arms and not on his in-jured body. Then my lips brushed against his. Both of his arms wrapped tightly around me as he kissed me back. Love overflowed from my heart, washing away my guilt over wasted time.

When Remi stirred, Preston released me, and I sat up.

"Yes, Hetty Clark, I accept your proposal."

A grin spread across his sweet lips.

"Does this mean you're getting me a ring?" He winked at me.

"Whatever it takes to convince you to marry me," I said.

"Just your feisty green eyes and warm kisses are all I need." He wiggled his eyebrows.

I smiled and stood.

"Now, get some rest. You've got to get better if you're gonna stand at Deacon's wedding and then ours."

He beamed brighter than the sun as I picked up Remi and closed the door behind me.

CHAPTER 32

December 23, 1893

PRESTON

"Are you fine taking care of the horses for a few more weeks?" I asked my posse.

"Are you kidding?" Brian asked. "Of course, we'll take care of them. You go."

"Enjoy the visit with your family," Clyde said.

"Don't worry about things," Rich said.

"When is your wedding?" Iris asked.

Not soon enough. "New Year's Day," I answered.

"Alright, we'll see you soon," Thomas said.

He handed Ranger's reins to the stock car attendant. Then he gave him the reins for White Lightning.

"Riding in style," he teased.

"It was nice of James to loan us his private car," Tildy said as she boarded the two-car train.

"Wow!" Hetty exclaimed as she entered.

I followed her and thought her exclamation failed to describe the ornate car. Plush chairs sat next to side tables. Dark wood covered the bottom half of the walls, while gold wallpaper covered the top half. Red velvet curtains framed the windows. Nervously, I sat in one of the cushioned chairs, afraid I might get it dirty.

"This is so nice," Tildy said.

Remi sat on the floor, unaware of his splendid surroundings, as he played with Brandy. Bringing the dog caused a minor argument between his mother and me. For once, I won.

Not that winning mattered. In nine days, she would become my wife at last. Nothing compared to that.

I shifted in the chair.

"Do you want to lie down?" Hetty asked. "The couch looks pretty comfy."

I gave her my roguish smile. "Not alone."

Pink brushed the apples of her cheeks. "Nine days."

"I'm pretty sure snuggling is allowed before then."

She tried to scowl, but her eyes sparkled.

"Go lay down," she said.

For once, I listened to her.

Before I knew it, the train slowed, and the engineer stopped it where the tracks crossed Colter land. I appreciated it. Normally, the ride from town took almost an hour. Disembarking on Colter land meant only a few more minutes of travel.

When I reached down to pick up Brandy, Hetty scolded me. "Don't lift her. She's too heavy."

"Relax. Doctor said I'm fine."

"And not to lift anything heavy."

I rolled my eyes as she picked up Brandy and set her in the basket I rigged up behind my saddle on Ranger. After Hetty mounted White Lightning, I handed Remi to her. When I helped Tildy up to her horse, Hetty frowned at me, but held her tongue.

Then I mounted Ranger, and we rode across the pastures of my childhood home. Nostalgia settled over me. I wanted to see my family. And to stand at Deacon's wedding.

When I wrote to him about Hetty and that we wanted to marry on New Year's Day, I was worried it was too close to his wedding. He told me the only reason he waited so long to marry Lilian was because she wanted a Christmas Day wedding. He wholeheartedly approved of our chosen wedding day.

The meaning of the day was special to us. A new year to represent a fresh start in our relationship. We looked forward to the future instead of over our shoulders at the painful past. At the start of the year, we would be a real family at last.

"It looks so different from this direction," Hetty said as she pulled up next to me.

"But just as comforting."

She laughed. "Race you!"

Before I could answer, she kicked her horse into a gallop.

"No fair," I said to Tildy.

Tildy laughed. "Sometimes she doesn't play fair. She knows you can't ride fast with Brandy on the back."

Brandy started whining the further away Remi moved with his mother. I pushed Ranger for a nice trot, though my back complained a little.

When we pulled to a stop in front of the ranch house, Brandy whined more.

"Stay."

I dismounted. Then I turned, and she jumped into my arms before she jumped to the ground a second later. When she stood next to Remi, she licked his hand. The sight filled me with joy.

A cowboy helped Tildy down. Then he took our horses to the barn. It seemed strange someone other than Deacon and Grady offered to care for them.

"How are you feeling?" Hetty asked as she looped her arm around my waist.

"Excited."

"I mean, your back."

"Well enough."

We filled the next hour with greetings and settling into the rooms at Aunt Julia's house. Deacon's future wife and sisters were staying at the Larson's old house, which they nicknamed the lodge. Her brothers stayed in the bunkhouse. Only Adam and Julia had room for us.

We didn't mind. We enjoyed the time with them. I even sneaked in some conversations about the stables.

As Christmas Day came, my excitement grew. Deacon's nerves became apparent quickly. He rearranged all the chairs in his house. When he headed over to the lodge in the morning, Lilian sent him back to his house with a warning not to enter the building before their wedding. My job was to keep him away from the lodge.

About an hour before the wedding, Boone and James arrived with their families. Grady came out the night before with his wife, Lilian's sister.

I headed over to the lodge with the rings in my pocket. I wore a suit at Deacon's request. It was the same one I'd wear in a few days for my wedding.

My gaze scanned the lodge until I spotted Hetty. I smiled, and she smiled back. I hoped she awaited our special day as much as I did.

"James!" Papa stuck his head in the doorway. "Deacon needs help with his tie."

James laughed and followed Papa over to Deacon's

house. A few minutes later, the three of them entered the lodge. Then Deacon took his place at the front while I stood next to him and Grady next to me.

When I caught Deacon rubbing his thumb over his index finger, I said, "Relax."

He stuffed his hand in his pocket.

"Thanks for coming," he said. "It means a lot to all of us."

"Thanks for asking me to stand for you." I squeezed his shoulder. "I'm glad you did."

He gave me a sharp nod. Then his eyes looked past me. His face softened as I slid into my place.

The ceremony flew by. My big brother, Deacon, was married. To a woman that loved him completely.

My day was right around the corner.

Hetty and I walked around the lake after the ceremony. We whispered words of love and hope to each other. I hoped the days would fly by. I wanted her in my arms forever.

CHAPTER 33

January 1, 1894

HETTY

Today, my restless wrangler would become my husband. I would take his name. Hetty Colter. I smirked. Wouldn't even have to change the initials on my saddle. Preston would laugh at that.

Colter.

I remembered back to the first time I met him at the Cow-boy Tournament. I did not know what love was. Infatuation, yes, and I had it bad for the skinny bronc rider with the intense blue eyes.

Nor did I know where our attraction would lead. Thinking of those nights with him in 1890, when Remi was conceived, brought bittersweet feelings. I loved my son, and he brought me tremendous joy. Yet, the direction my relationship with Preston took brought equal heartache.

The day Preston showed up at Clark Ranch, asking for a job, I wanted to wring his neck and find a preacher all at the same time. That would have been a mistake. We needed time to get to know each other.

I sighed as Mama held up my dress. A fancy dress for my man. It wasn't a white dress like some women wore these days. It was a dress I'd wear on Sundays or on a special date with Preston. The pale green silk glimmered in the afternoon sun filtering through the window. When it settled on my shoulders, I ran my fingers over the soft material. Fancy indeed.

"He's going to pass out when he stops breathing after seeing you in this," Mama teased.

"Does he know about the posse?" I asked.

"Don't think so. We've kept it a surprise."

"Will we have room for them and his brothers at the front?"

With Clyde officiating, we still needed space for seven men, his four brothers, and the three other posse members. It would look odd, especially since I only had Vi and Iris standing for me.

"We'll make it work."

"Should we ask Grady?"

Mama shook her head. "He thinks the day should be about his brothers."

I sighed. "My hair seems limp to me."

Mama laughed. "Are you nervous?"

"No." I lied.

"We're here!" Vi said as she breezed into the room. "Here, let me fix your hair."

After what seemed like forever, Vi finally dubbed my hair finished. Then she pushed me in front of a mirror. I hardly recognized myself. I looked stunning. Feminine. Fancy dress worthy.

"Is it time?" I asked as my hand shook.

"Almost," Iris said. "Come on, Violet. Let's go take our places."

Once they left, Mama stood before me. She placed her hand on my cheek.

"Today would thrill your father. He'd be proud, too."

My eyes burned.

"I'm convinced he knew exactly who he rescued in that fire," Mama said. Then she tapped my nose. "It was you."

"Stop, you'll make me cry."

She kissed my cheek. Then she clasped my hand and led me to the lodge.

I cracked the door open and watched as Preston's brothers took their places next to him. They decided on reverse birth order, so James stood on the end furthest from Preston. Then the posse made their presence known. Preston's eyes turned red. Each of them hugged him before they stood next to James. When Rich approached, Preston grabbed his hand and pulled him to the front of the line. The two men became such close friends after Preston left my ranch.

My heart warmed. Soon it would be our ranch. We have already planned to move Larson Stables out to Clark Ranch.

As I remembered asking Preston about the ranch's name, I smiled. I asked if we should rename it to Colter Ranch.

"Absolutely not. We honor your father's legacy by keeping his name on the ranch."

However, we had legal paperwork drawn up to make Remi officially his son. Remington Matthew Clark Colter. A big name for a small boy. One day he'd grow into it.

As the men settled into place, Iris entered. Clyde moved to the front next to Preston. Then I entered.

My gaze locked on Preston's as his eyes widened. Then he swallowed hard. Will Colter offered me his arm as he stood in for my father.

When I stood across from him, Preston whispered in my ear. "You are Hetty Clark, right?"

I laughed. "Yes."

He winked at me. "Good. I wanted to make sure I married the prettiest woman in all of Arizona."

I smiled as we said our vows. We took our time and spoke them deliberately to each other. Vows we would keep forever, with the help of our Lord, family, and posse.

Then Clyde announced us as Mr. and Mrs. Preston Colter. And Remi Colter.

My heart pounded as Preston pulled me tight against him. Then his lips captured mine. He kissed me with a little heat, and I enjoyed every second.

He pulled back, and whispered, "No more 'shouldn'ts'."

I laughed. "You're evil."

"And I'm all yours. Forever."

Then I walked down the aisle holding my husband's arm while he held our son's hand. We made the best-looking family around.

EPILOGUE

Clark Ranch
Near Ash Fork, Arizona Territory
April 24, 1898

PRESTON

How many people could we fit in our house? I wondered as more friends and family arrived by the minute. It was a special day at Clark Ranch.

My five-year anniversary. I smiled. The entire thing had been Hetty's idea. Besides our wedding anniversary, this day was the most important day in our family's life, in my life.

Under normal circumstances, it was nearly impossible to say no to my lovely wife. Certainly wasn't gonna say no to this. She was right.

"Five years," Rich said as he hugged me. "That is quite an accomplishment."

"Eight for you now, right?" Brian asked.

Rich nodded.

"Fifteen for Clyde. Almost sixteen," Brian added. He seemed to be the official recordkeeper.

"Three for you, Mark. And Thomas is at... Almost seven."

Both men nodded. I glanced over at Chester. His shoulders slumped. I squeezed his shoulder.

"Five months is good. Today's celebration should give you hope. It is possible to change."

Chester nodded.

My papa greeted me with a hug. "Five years, son. I'm so proud of you."

"How long has it been for you?" I asked him.

He puffed his cheeks and blew out a long breath. "I am not sure how long. Let's see. I've been married to your mother for thirty-four years. So probably around thirty-seven?"

"We should have this party for you."

Papa laughed. "Thanks for having us up."

"Fritz!" Hetty yelled. "Settle down."

"Telling a two-year-old Colter to settle down is like asking the sun not to rise," Boone said. "Especially if he's one of yours."

I laughed. He had a good point, though our second son took after his mother. Wouldn't listen to a soul and was the feistiest kid in the territory. She said he took after me, but we all knew the truth.

Sam, Ellie Mae, and their five children arrived. I greeted each by name. Sterling, Brody, Ashley, Riley, and Scarlett, the baby. They might be finished expanding their family, since Scarlett just turned three. Then again, Vi surprised Mama eight years after me.

James greeted me.

"Did you reserve an entire train for this gaggle?" I teased him.

"I don't think there were too many passengers who were

not Colters."

His wife, Keri, greeted me with a hug. They had two children, Tate and Geneva. I wondered if more were on the way soon.

Then Jaclyn, Boone's wife, hugged me. "Sorry. Wrangling Jaxson…"

"Say nothing more. He is the spitting image of Boone, so I understand."

"Autumn, this is your uncle Preston."

A sweet, dark-haired girl smiled shyly. Her amber eyes sparkled with a hint of mischief.

"Preston!" Vi came up and hugged me for a solid minute.

My little sister still hadn't found her soulmate. Her first attempt left her at the altar. Both Hetty and I prayed she'd find happiness one day. She would be an amazing mother, just like ours.

Mama came up and kissed my cheek. "So many people."

"Most of them are your kin," I teased her.

"I know. I say the same thing on holidays, and we rarely have everyone show up."

Hetty came up next to me and looped an arm around my waist.

"Hannah, so good to see you."

After Mama hugged her, she returned her arm to my waist.

"Can I talk to you for a minute?"

"Sure."

"Alone?"

She took my hand and led me into her office.

"Preston, I just wanted to say I'm so proud of you for staying sober for five years."

My heart melted.

"I'm sorry it took me so long to understand."

I pulled her into my arms. "Hush now. Today is a happy day."

"But, I wish—"

I placed a finger on her lips. "We had a bumpy start to our relationship. None of it matters. We've enjoyed over four years of wedded bliss."

She snorted, as she knew the truth. Some of it was blissful. Some of it was painful. We faced challenges. We celebrated joys. It was as normal as the next marriage. At least that's what Iris reassured us.

"You look nice, by the way," I said as I wiggled my eyebrows.

"In britches and a faded work shirt?"

"Too bad we weren't in the bedroom. I'd help you pick out a different outfit then."

"Preston!"

I cut anything else she might have said short as I kissed my gorgeous wife. It was my favorite way to celebrate.

AUTHOR'S NOTE

When writing a series about five sons, I wanted to make each of their personalities different. Their strengths and weak-nesses varied. And, well, every multi-sibling family always seems to have that one sibling that differs completely from the rest. Preston is that Colter son. As I mapped out the series, sketched the characters, and chose titles for the books, the title "Restless Wrangler" came to mind. It was the true inspiration for Preston's character. I asked, what would earn a man that moniker?

By far, my favorite part of Preston's story was his home-coming to the ranch as a changed man. The prodigal para-ble told by Jesus in Luke 15:11-32 is dear to me as I spent my early twenties as a prodigal. Though the details of Pres-ton's story differ from my own, the feelings his character expresses matched my experience. The good news is that Jesus can redeem any broken part of our pasts if we let Him.

It was fun writing Hetty Clark's character, such a strong woman who made a few mistakes that changed the direc-tion of her life. Isn't that how life goes? My primary inspira-tion for her character came from a few articles I read on the Sharlot Hall Museum's online archives about the earliest ro-deos ("Cowboy Tournaments") in Prescott. It surprised me to learn that there were women's events as early as 1889, though they were probably sidesaddle riding events and not bronco riding. The article even named the seven women contestants. None of them were named Hetty, but the name seemed to fit with other names of the period.

One of the more recent research tools I've discovered is the online archive for Chronicling America. On this site, you can search for newspaper articles from any town for any date. I found several articles specifically about the Independence Day celebration in Prescott from newspapers published in 1893, which advertised the Cowboy Tournament, baseball, horse races, bicycle race, shooting matches, a ball in the evening, and more. Throughout the series, I've woven in different aspects of the celebration. Also, you may wonder why I include Independence Day in many of my books. It's because this holiday and the rodeo have always been the event of the year for the town of Prescott, even to this day.

You may or may not have noticed that books 3, 4, and 5 overlap the timeline. Book 3 follows James's story from 1891 to 1893. All of Deacon's story in book 4 occurred during 1893. And Preston's story spanned April 1893 to January 1894. The main reason I included Preston's story in 1893 was because of the Ash Fork fire I wrote into book 3. I knew it provided the perfect catalyst for Preston's "rock bottom" to motivate his life change.

I hope you enjoyed Preston and Hetty's story.

Since I wrote in a surprise daughter for Will and Hannah in book 1, I've included Violet's story as part of the Colter Sons Series. Read her story in: *The Resilient Bride (Colter Sons Book 6)*.

Karen Baney

Want More Arizona Territory Romance?

Get a FREE novella featuring characters connected to the Colter Sons series! Plus exclusive updates on new releases, special offers, and historical insights from the frontier.

Subscribe at: books.karenbaney.com/larson-christmas

ABOUT THE AUTHOR

Karen Baney is passionate about writing stories full of flawed characters. She enjoys weaving together stories of second chances, redemption, and overcoming personal trials. As a transplant to Arizona, she loves researching the state's history and finding ways to seamlessly incorporate real history and real settings into her novels. In addition to writing and speaking, Karen works as a Software Development Manager for a Christian ministry.

Her faith plays an important role both in her life and in her writing. Karen and her husband, Jim, make their home in Gilbert, Arizona, with their two dogs, Bella and Daisy. Both Jim and Karen are active at Rock Point Church in Queen Creek, Arizona.

Discover faith-laced stories with characters who feel like lifelong friends.

Visit www.karenbaney.com to discover more historical romance series set in the American West. Follow Karen's writing journey and get behind-the-scenes glimpses of her research adventures on social media.

Facebook:	@AuthorKarenBaney
X:	@karen_baney
Instagram:	@AuthorKarenBaney
BookBub:	Follow Karen Baney for new release alerts

BOOKS BY KAREN BANEY

Historical Western Romance

Prescott Pioneers Series:
Step back in time to the wild, untamed Arizona Territory where survival depends on grit, faith, and the courage to start over. Follow three pioneer families—the Andersons, Colters, and Larsons—as they risk everything for the promise of a new life in a land that demands both strength and hope.

A Dream Unfolding
A Heart Renewed
A Life Restored
A Hope Revealed
Hidden Prospects

Desert Manna Series:
Sometimes the most beautiful love stories bloom in the desert. Set in the growing frontier town of Prescott during the early 1870s, these tender romances follow women rebuilding their lives after heartbreak and the unexpected men who help them discover that second chances at love are worth the risk. Set in Prescott, Arizona between 1871 - 1873.

Beauty for Ashes
Joy for Mourning
Oaks of Justice

Colter Sons Series:
Power, legacy, and forbidden love collide in this sweeping family saga set in the Arizona Territory. The Colter ranch

empire has weathered decades of frontier life, but now family secrets and buried betrayals threaten to destroy everything. As five brothers—and one resilient sister—navigate the treacherous waters of love, loss, and redemption, they must decide what's worth fighting for. Set in Prescott and other locations within the Arizona Territory in 1887 - 1906.

The Reluctant Cattleman
The Roaming Adventurer
The Railroad Magnate
The Resourceful Stockman
The Restless Wrangler
The Resilient Bride

Larson Sisters Series
Meet the next generation! These delightful novellas follow the three daughters of Adam and Julia Larson from the *Prescott Pioneers Series* as they navigate love, courtship, and finding their own happily ever afters in territorial Arizona in 1886 – 1894.

In Love at Christmas
In Love with the Rancher
In Love with the Horse Trainer

Contemporary Romance

Vargas Ranch Series:
Love is in the air at the Vargas Guest Ranch & Resort near Wickenburg, Arizona. Meet the Vargas family—five swoon-worthy brothers and their cousins who live by their family motto: "We do not deviate from the Lord's plan."

These rugged cowboys run a successful working ranch and luxury resort while navigating the rollercoaster of finding true love.

Falling for a Fake Cowboy
Falling for a Real Cowboy
Honeymoon with a Real Cowboy
Falling for a Shy Cowboy
Falling for a Bossy Cowboy
Falling for a Smart Cowboy
Falling for a Humbug Cowboy
Falling for a Devoted Cowgirl
Falling for a Pregnant Cowgirl
Falling for a Cowboy's Legacy

Steadfast Love Series:

The *Steadfast Love* series follows a close-knit group of friends as they navigate the beautiful mess of modern life in the Phoenix area—workplace drama, complicated families, and love that shows up when they least expect it. These contemporary romances blend emotional depth with authentic faith, reminding us that even when life unravels, God's love never does.

The Heart I Rescue (prequel)
The Air I Breathe

Jilted, abandoned, and widowed. I never planned on falling in love again.

My third attempt at marriage left me a widow…
and a single mother.

My name is Violet (Colter) Gamble, and I told God I'm giving up on love. I don't need a husband.

Or so I thought. The man who bullied me in school shows up and struggles to raise his daughter alone, giving us common ground.

Then an unexpected shock sends me spiraling. He is ready to help me. I want to lean on him, only I don't think I can without losing my heart.

Will I stick to my resolve or cave in to give love a fourth try?

———

If you love emotionally rich Christian romance with rugged frontier grit…

Janette Oke meets Louis L'Amour. Mary Connealy meets Zane Grey.

The *Colter Sons* series blends heartfelt faith journeys, masculine coming-of-age arcs, and sweeping Arizona history into unforgettable love stories.

DESERT LIFE MEDIA

———

Desert Life Media: *There Is Life in The Desert*

Entertainment-first Christian fiction set in the Southwest, featuring redemption, family, and faith

Publishing clean, wholesome, and uplifting fiction since 2010

———

desertlifemedia.com